PHARMAKON

Almudena Sánchez (Mallorca, 1985) is a journalist and writer living in Madrid. Her debut collection of stories *La acústica de los iglús* / *The Acoustics of Igloos* (Caballo de Troya, 2016), was finalist for the Ojo Crítico and Setenil prizes. Since the 2021 publication of *Pharmakon*, Sánchez is a frequent contributor to media and events focused on mental health issues, speaking with candor and humor about her personal experience.

Katie Whittemore is a translator from Spanish. Her translations include *Four by Four* and *Bad Handwriting* by Sara Mesa (Open Letter Books), *The Communist's Daughter* by Aroa Moreno Durán (Tinder Press), *World's Best Mother* by Nuria Labari (World Editions), *Wolfskin* by Lara Moreno (Structo Press and Open Letter Books), *Last Words on Earth* by Javier Serena (Open Letter Books), *Mother's Don't* by Katixa Agirre (Open Letter Books), and *The Strangers* by Jon Bilbao (Dalkey Archive).

This translation has been published in Great Britain
by Fum d'Estampa Press Limited 2023
001

© Almudena Sánchez Jiménez, 2021
This edition is published by arrangement with
CASANOVAS & LYNCH LITERARY AGENCY S.L.
All rights reserved.

English language translation © Katie Whittemore, 2023

The moral rights of the author and translator have been asserted
Set in Minion Pro

Printed and bound by Great Britain by CMP UK Ltd.
A CIP catalogue record for this book is available from the British Library

ISBN: 978-1-913744-20-5

This publication was supported by a grant from Acción Cultural Española (AC/E)

PHARMAKON

ALMUDENA SÁNCHEZ

Translated by

KATIE WHITTEMORE

PHARMAKON

People struggle on the bed or on
the floor, neither alive nor dead.
JUAN-EDUARDO CIRLOT
88 sueños

With so many secrets, obviously I
had to end up writing.
CAMILA SOSA VILLADA
El viaje inútil

I will not fail at patience.
ROSA BERBEL
Las niñas siempre dicen la verdad

VERTIGO OVERLOAD

Speaking of heads: it's about time we started blowing some up. Fewer explosions in Lebanon and more in our Western minds. The world would be a better place if heads were prepared to harbor anti-bias bombs. Collateral damage: empathy. But who am I to give orders? I'm just a writer starting out. I'll always be a writer starting out. In 2087, I'll still be that writer—starting out, trembling, daring, trembling still, fork in hand.

People can do whatever they want with their heads. In the end, they're all we have. Thinking heads. My own head exploded and here I am telling that story, with no intention of writing a general interest or self-help piece and taking great pains for this book to contain more literature than grounds for morbid curiosity, more literature than technical facts, more literature than anything that isn't literature. Put more simply: I want my depression to be as literary as my life has been ever since I learned how to read.

Reading is the best thing that ever happened to me: to read well, to read calmly, assiduously. To read the blank line that follows the written one and the written line that precedes the blank. To read and dream, read and digest, read and revere, read on the verge of tears. Read and weave in my own words, a disruption of the senses.

I didn't believe in it at first. I didn't believe in depression or "the blues" or OCD or panic attacks. They felt foreign. Temporary foolishness. All my life, I'd been taught that depression was just people needing *to snap out of it* or *to pull themselves together*. People *blowing things out of proportion*. Like all preconceptions, I guess, it's been hard for me to detonate this thing in my head.

I've read marvelous things related to the brain's collapse. Fever forces growth: we flourish on fever, fever and more fever.

Good books have a temperature of about 103 degrees. Which is the elevated temperature you might experience with altitude sickness. The body close to death. Delirium. Vertigo overload. It's when we most resemble the Devil and that, too, is depression.

Suddenly, we find ourselves fragile and aflame.

So as to not simply rely on transcendental episodes from my childhood (I haven't suffered any recent tragedy), I've written about my failure to write (it's my job, after all) when my depression proved most severe. It often pained me to think about the halcyon days when writing flowed through me more easily. When I was a writer with the will to be one. It's terrible to lose your desire: the deadliest thing I've ever experienced. For months I believed—and this I swear—that I would never, never-ever, write again.

In childhood, there is a sea. A sea altered by memory, of course, but I've gone back and compared pieces of these recollections with those of my brother and my aunt Antonina— both of whom agree with me, more or less—and with my parents, who do not agree at all. I've spent an abnormal amount of time studying pictures of myself as a little girl. Up close, with a magnifying glass. From a distance, through binoculars. Holding my heart in my hands, holding ashes. I'm smiling in very few of the pictures. In some of them, I look like I wonder what I'm doing there. Why's this girl in the picture with a question on her face?

Childhood precedes memory.

I'm convinced that when I die, if I do die one of these days, it won't be my life flashing before my eyes but my entire childhood, my underwater childhood, my rotten childhood, my childhood spent in a car driving up one street and down another, out to one end of the island, through the fields of Castille, thirsty and dizzy from the smell of petrol.

Writing is akin to water. Writers (as Cheever presaged) swim in different bodies of water. There are many kinds of water. So many textures. So many colors. I'm increasingly convinced: I write water, I want my texts to flow. The imitation of water is key.

I drink water with lemon and ginger every morning to start the day right.

Is this really something in my genes that can't be controlled? My psychiatrist talks to me very seriously about this, about *the endogenous*. About how my depression is unavoidable, how I can't blame myself, I can't blame myself and could I please, please not blame myself. And I started thinking about my grandmother. About a grandmother I never knew. About an unhappy grandmother I once had.

Pharmakon is written backwards.

Let me clarify: it's written forwards and backwards, backwards and forwards. Like when we used to hit rewind during a movie. I really miss being able to do that. Pressing the button on the remote control, making the people on screen go crazy. It was funny, watching them walk backwards out the door. In reverse. Their butts popping off a chair, almost in flight. The rewind button probably inspired magical realism, right? How ever did we start flying around in books? I don't think the current mood is amenable to us messing with our characters like that.

Rewinding was a way of disrupting the world, the sacred rules of the good life.

We don't have this button anymore. You can view the previous scene or the next one, the fifteen seconds before or fifteen seconds after. Soon, even remote controls will cease to exist.

Sometimes I think we're important we humans who have lived both before and after the dawn of the internet. And when we disappear, there will be no one left to witness the cataclysm. Planet Earth festers with megabytes, fake profiles, Wi-Fi. It's like living both before and after the invention of the wheel.

My mother complains she isn't tech-savvy. But I would need two hundred pages to delve into my mother—a whole novel. My mother is very much like Enriqueta's mother in the Linier comics. Enriqueta's mother is both never and always there. In fact, she never appears physically drawn. I have an omnibus of Liniers's work and Enriqueta's mother is always just a shouting voice. My own mother is like God: I never see her, but she sees me.

That's what God is, right? Omnipresent.

Maybe God is mothers.

I'm interested in those sorts of phantom presences. In some ways, we owe an interesting childhood to our parents: to what they did at the time and what they stopped doing. I absolutely do not mean to blame them. Just the opposite, really: this book is so they understand me a little better. For them to read my point of view.

My point of view, which starts inside a wound and ends with a kiss on the new skin growing over it; my lips might be chapped but I kiss my baggage, I kiss it day and night. It's me: I have to keep kissing myself in order to properly heal. Don't wait for someone to kiss you. Kiss yourself.

I'm opposed to Walt Disney and in favor of pharmacies.

Long live chemistry and long live Effexor. Long live the white powders that brighten our existence, the ibuprofen that rescues me from occassional but nightmarish sciatica, long live dried passion fruit extract, whatever. Even my cat gets wasted on valerian and writhes around on the floor! I'm more chummy than ever with these pills. I swallow them without thinking, without fear. I used to have my qualms but I've realized they're no big deal: they only make you better. Four, five, six pills a day. I sound like an old lady, talking about analgesics and their effect on serotonin. I know I do. And yet, I look young. I'm very much like my mother in this respect; why deny it.

Inside, I'm a child: I ramble, play in the park with the other kids, swing from the monkey bars like a regressed primate. I'll never give up these silly things. Not like anybody sees me, anyway.

My childhood is now. Childhood is whenever one wants it to be and for me it's come at the age of thirty-three. Until I turned ten, I was something else: an earthquake simulation.

In the filmography of your life, what matters is how you are seen. And how much damage you can do to yourself if you aren't.

We are creatures in plain sight.

In plain sight of God.

Suicide is a moment of non-thought. It is an act carried out with one's heart in boiling water, like a lobster. You aren't fully aware of it until your feet are off the ground, until you're gone from the earth, because to die is to not be. To not participate. You'll be talked about and you won't able to interject. You'll see a bright-eyed boy and won't hug him. You can't do anything. Suicide is prohibition.

The substances I've ingested (such thirst for pills that cure) have changed my body and my face.

And my soul. (Sorry.)

I've lost weight, gained weight, lost it again. I went from 145 pounds to 100 in a year and a half.

I've passed out three times. Once I was at a Starbucks on the nubby floor mat where people wipe their feet. My head was almost trampled. My partner rushed me out of there as if shielding a treasure he was in danger of losing: his dignity.

Everything that makes our heart race is wonderful. Tenderness. Sophisticated conversation accompanied by anchovies. Two thousand inconspicuous kisses on your face. Feline ears poking your chest. Eventually, the heart will slow. The thing is to have catalysts nearby that can speed it up for you.

This book is for sad people with a sense of humor who, at some point in their lives, noticed that their brain was leaving them, that it was slipping through their hands when our hands are—realistically—the human parts we use to grab hold of the most delicate things and hug them to us, hug them tight.

I've placed a thermometer in the pages of this book.

BANANA

I was six years old the first time I thought about death. My foot, an object worthy of study, had gotten caught between the back wheel and the chain guard of my bike.

The bike was a Christmas present from my parents—dressed as, in 1993, as the Three Wisemen—and it had been an issue because they hadn't known where to hide it; it wasn't exactly a discreet present and I almost caught them adjusting the handlebar or wrapping it or something.

Anyway, soon Almudena will have a growth spurt and we'll just have to get her a new one with gears and a kilometer counter.

It's hard to explain. How I got my ankle in there. How I jammed it in, so twisted.

Come on now, rotate it, Almudena. Let's see.

I could still walk if I dragged the bike with me, but that wasn't the problem. My ankle had decided to separate from my body: the first corporeal cleavage in my life. I'm not sure which parent grew so hysterical that the following occurred to them: my father went away and came back with a giant saw. I've seen a lot of sharpened saws throughout my life—woodcutters', butchers'— although none with such deep teeth as that big old rake.

At the sight of my father approaching with the hacksaw, I started to run with the bike: away, away, trying to get away. No, papá, no! No, papá, please! Mamá, tell him no! I can live with the bike on my leg, I'll go to school like this. I swear it on our house!

It was a wood chipper. He started cutting at the chainguard shackling me to the vehicle.

Despite this, I like bikes. Mechanical apparatus, on the other hand, I find unpleasant. Cameras are complicated, with their diaphragms and panoramic zooms. I'm drawn to steam-operated machines, like popcorn poppers or air crispers: the fireworks of food. Sewing machines are scary: my mother once told me how she pricked her finger one night making a hat for someone's baby who had been born deaf. No, blind. The baby couldn't see well: all staticky.

After that, I imagined her as a twenty-first century Sleeping Beauty.

Vacuums, well, I find those unsettling: absorbers of filth. And the most dreaded objects: pool drains. I was an excellent underwater swimmer when I was little. My friends were good swimmers, but I was the only one who knew how to store air deep inside. I had my own theory: too much talking is a waste of air, but I went around listening and obeying with my big healthy lungs. I was happy in the pool, in my low-oxygen world, until I learned that a girl had lost her arm while swimming down really deep: the pool drain sucked it off. Her arm. Practically swallowed it whole. I stopped swimming underwater. I stopped going near any kind of suction. I didn't let boys give me hickeys. The mere thought of kissing them and being kissed terrified me. Took me years to get over it. Some of them called me a dyke, a carpet muncher. Other boys, the more sensitive ones, called me perversely shy.

Adolescence was my steep mountain to climb. My fiery peak. In high school, they referred to this period as "Introduction to Adult Life." Introduction what? A class? I was worried about infinity: the bumps on the wall, the financial bubble, whether or not the bottom of my shoe smelled like dog poop. This book is about childhood, fiendish childhood, beginning with a bike and ending with vomit. Like most childhoods, right?

I like biking because it precedes driving and I was always good at that, at getting around. This was my route: from the port in Andratx to the lighthouse, from the lighthouse to the kiosk, from the kiosk to the port, from the port to the roundabout, from the roundabout to the lighthouse, etc., etc.

Small places are good for raising children. They're defined. I don't understand maps. Between Pinto and Valdemoro, I drew an angry octopus.

To write your thoughts is to begin to live them.

I was scared of the saw. My foot swelled and stung: my parents and I sweat in unison, convoluted sweat and tears, raw flesh, weird fluid leaking from the saw.

What's this bike made out of, methacrylate? my parents asked, heads in their hands.

What's coming out of the saw? Is that water? I demanded an immediate answer.

Oil?

My mother was the one who threw her hands up most. She got stuck that way, I think. Hands on her head.

Almudena, you'll rip my skin off, squeezing my hand like that. Please.

I want to know if that's water coming out of the saw!

I specialize in terrified interjections.

My childhood home has gargoyles. It looks like Notre Dame. Clay shaped into mythical creatures. A garden needs decorating:

Which do you prefer? Gargoyles or gnomes?

I chose the gargoyles and they brought monsters. I really regret it. I imagined, I don't know, a toucan.

Our house—the one with the gargoyles—is in a housing development in Mallorca and in the 1990s, we were the only Spaniards. All of our neighbors were foreigners. My screams were getting louder and my father's fury intensifying, reflected in the saw and the muscles of his face.

A neighbor casually strolled in through the garage door and exclaimed in English:

Good morning!

My mother intervened:

Almudena, someone is speaking to you. Be polite and say hi.

I said a tearful hello to the neighbor and then erupted with a supersonic truth:

I'm going to die! I'm going to die!

Nobody else remembers this, but I would testify to it under oath: the foreign neighbor, amidst all the commotion (my foot was still completely jammed), brought me a peeled banana, pointing directly up at the sky. It wasn't a regular banana, and the saw wasn't a saw, and my house wasn't my house. A young girl does not forget these things.

A banana. Phallic and creamy.

I watched the banana with anxious eyes. If it could've, the banana would have howled.

Look, Almudena, how thoughtful, do you want a banana?

It was my mother speaking: she's always the speaker, though my father also says words. No, I said, half-drowned in tears, and the neighbor made an expression of profound disappointment. He continued to insist with the banana and I managed to get a couple more screams in, containing a specific plea:

I don't want a banana! I'm going to die! No banana! Get out them out of here, the man and the banana!

The afternoon passed as afternoons do: it filled up. My father finally cut through the chain guard and felt powerful. My mother struck up a conversation with the neighbor, apologizing for my attitude and the fact that I didn't eat his banana. I sat a while and observed my foot. Between my ankle and heel, a negligible mark was developing.

Insignificant, a doctor declared.

Nonetheless, from close-up or faraway, the mark is shaped like a scythe.

DIAGNOSIS

My sentimental education is summarized in a single paragraph:

Be pretty and pay your dues. Don't let yourself go, look nice, never give up and if somebody tries to bring you down, breeze right past them. Don't say yes, don't say no, leave things on standby, and if they demand an answer, tell them you're doing your own thing and nobody else's. Lastly: misery loves company. In terms of material things, be both frugal and worldly. Culture, for instance: saying "Tutankhamen was a pharaoh belonging to Egypt's XVIII dynasty" or "Plutonium is a radioactive transuranic element, its chemical symbol is Pu," implies a sign of greatness. Accrue culture, smile, amaze the audience.

I never received any advice about fear, maladjustment, shock, or mental brutality. And I needed it so badly. In my town, Andratx, there were people who had the blues or even worse; they were off their rocker, off their head. And just how should the head hang, I wondered. Straight? Now that I think about it, I do have a long neck and I move it around a lot. If I look up the word *depression* online, everything is depression. It is a rounded word, multipurpose, sadness will pass, cured with a kiss. It's gets thrown around. I can't go to the pool today, I have a family lunch—be depressed for me. The store's out of Grefusa and Frit Ravich caramel-covered peanuts, so depressing. My lens cloth is at home, I'll have to clean these dirty glasses with my breath, gross, I'm getting depressed. A person gets depressed on Christmas Eve and carves a turkey.

Right now, I'm writing heavily medicated with antidepressants and this book is starting to take shape.

I want to define an abstract state. I'm getting better and I don't have a scar to show that I've been through something horrible. It was a slow decline. I went from sleeping in my bed to on the couch. It was exhausting, the idea of making the bed every day. I thought I'd made a brilliant decision: blanket, couch, TV. I thought: It'll just be a few nights, five or six, until I'm back to my old vibrant self. The living room became my only chamber. I didn't leave it: living room to bathroom, bathroom to living room.

This initial change was followed by a cooking hiatus. I didn't need to eat much. My body demanded nothing but rest and gloom. I left the shades drawn in the morning and, at dusk, a handful—what am I saying! a stampede!—of tears tumbled when I saw the final flicker of the streetlights coming on outside.

I weighed the possibility that I was suffering a considerable crisis. I didn't like to look at myself in the mirror. My partner didn't deserve such a face, grey and hollow, because I wouldn't consent to a bite of food. I wanted to leave the relationship. My arms couldn't reach the highest supermarket shelves, so I stopped shopping. I would get buried under avalanches of Kellogg's cereal boxes, tinned sardines, and lupini beans. Everything ached. Fortunately, the compassionate clerks in the big box stores camouflaged the incident: it was just an accident. Some early mornings I got up and, still in pajamas, bundled myself into a coat and wandered the worst streets in Tetuán. I identified with the bedraggled, the gamblers, the homeless and clearly lost, backs to the sun. While I have a fairly existentialist spirit, my new routine was no innocent habit.

I left the phone off the hook so my parents couldn't reach me, their daughter in tatters: annihilated. I held a desert stone in my palm and prayed. I concentrated on the idea that somebody would realize what was wrong with me without me having to explain. What did I mean, what was wrong with me? That I didn't like grocery shopping? Nobody does! It's a pain in the ass. Get over it—do whatever you have to do. And what is that? What do you advise? What do you have, what can you arrange? What do you advocate? I wanted to vanish from this chore-ridden world, all of it so demanding. I was mocked by the dirty plates. Sauces dripped down the walls. You can't sense depression coming on. It starts at the forehead and moves to the knees. It is the biggest, most invisible, unexpected, destructive, selfish, unhealthy, paranoid, slobby, grimy, biased disease I've ever had. This is the sentence I heard most often:

Almudena, you are strong.

Strong how? A tree is strong enough to balance its branches, to support nests, wind, baby partridges, the woodpeckers that plonk themselves down and tap, tap, tap. Plagues of caterpillars. Ice storms. The death of an adjacent tree and the dry Manchegan summer. And yet there are trees that, for no reason, with no biological cause, rot from the inside. Experts will attest:

The bark is split. The trunk is twisted. This tree doesn't respond. Doesn't sprout. Weak roots. It could crack and fall on somebody. It must be chopped down.

In the five months that I have been depressed, I've also preferred to be chopped down. Into sections. Aren't screws sometimes put into categories? Threaded, round… well, I don't know anything about screws. I want to tell this in a way that doesn't come off as metaphorical. One day I wanted my head cut off; another day it was my arm, my foot, my stomach. A goddamn queasy stomach that, every day, every x number of hours, I had to fill, against my will, with food. Why does emptiness gather in the stomach? Why does it sound like thunder? I cannot stand the body's music: cramps, yawns, glup glup in the throat, gases, clicking jaws, zssssss.

The other day I read a Joy Williams story in which an alcoholic mother and her daughter take a trip to see a magic show. The magician is famous. They saw an ad in the paper and took interest. At some point during the act, the magician is about to saw a woman in two, at which point the mother erupts on stage, out of her mind, drunk, lurching. She wants to be the one cut in half. Sorry to ruin the story for anyone who hasn't read it, but in the end, security is called and they haul her off stage and take her to a nearby bar, where the mother continues to drink.

To rid myself of my demons, I go to a psychiatrist I'll call Dr. Magnus. I sit on a red couch. As a matter of fact, it isn't a couch: it is a rectangle of fears. The best and worst things have happened to me on a couch. The couch incites me, comforts me, relaxes my joints. There are no mirrors, but there is a jumble of photographs.

What's your plan? What have you thought about these past couple of weeks?

And I tell the psychiatrist: I get on a bus because I have abandoned the struggle. I'm retracting; I don't want to go forwards but back, really far back, to my birth, to before my birth: to the void. I get on a bus and I look at the passengers and I'm surprised. What are they doing on the bus? Traveling from one place to another? Why bother: we are all condemned. Sooner or later, we will die. We'll be eaten by worms, by the flies with their millimetric proboscis, by those nit things. I get it now. Why go on? Why does the driver participate in this comedy of mediocrity? How naïve, they got on a bus to go somewhere.

The news program ended while I was sitting and waiting for the will to use my fork to pick up a piece of steak. There is an unbreachable chasm between the fork and the steak. I would've almost preferred to eat it with my hands. They've falsified their Masters degrees, evaded the tax authorities, the retirees have protested and each segment is slightly entertaining: it's the only thing that moves my world, television moves me, occasionally I change the channel and it is an accomplishment; I've used the remote, my will desires something else, Antena 3 or *Criminal Minds*. The steak is still there, my aunt Antonina begs me to please take a bite. Matías Prats is speaking at the other end of the kitchen. He is a renowned Spanish newscaster, but he reverberates in my head like a ridiculous, failed creature stifling a sneeze. I want to change the channel, but it's hard: I have to get up, press a button, take a breath and then two steps, sit back down, wait to watch another cartoon of this unbearable life that is pushing me, pushing me softly and holding me back.

BITE

Before the incident with the bike—I'm not sure how many years before—I went to preschool. I was a quiet kid, I played on my own, chewed my hair, my fingernails, yawned, pinched myself, pulled off scabs, pulled out wiggly teeth, used my sleeve to wipe my boogers, pee, drool and puke, and occasionally ate bugs and dirt. They might've thought I suffered absence seizures. I think they sensed it. Once, I heard a chorus of whispers: *Bsbsbsbsbs*.

To get a picture of me for some official form, they had to do a whole photoshoot. As a child, I was already suspicious of adults and their chaotic presumptions. Early on, I knew that the important thing, the most crucial thing for survival, lay in listening to them. They think children don't hear, like, in general. In particular, they're sure that by the next day, the kids will have forgotten their reprimands and absolute truths—as if a kid were a blowfish! Well, no. Those things add up. It's called long-term memory.

Flashbacks, in fact, are the accumulation of childhood.

Among other things, I understood that language was a first-class weapon and that, in the future, I was going to be the queen of language and declare war on grown-ups: WWII, the Balkans, Vietnam, the Gulf. All the wars in encyclopedias.

And atlases.

History can be summed up by a war that becomes more sophisticated over time. Just yesterday an Arab sheik was subtly killed with a drone from the sky.

I would have my revenge for all the "I already said no," "because I said so," "eat this," "wear that," "you have to play the piano," "now's not the time for questions." I still feel as if I haven't yet beaten them in battle. I sense a quivering in my body. Like an out-of-sorts snow squall.

My preschool teacher was kind and flighty. There were a couple of kids with disabilities in my class. One of those kids—Xisco—had a habit of biting my left eye. Below my eyebrow, above my lashes, that's where he would take a big bite, like he was tearing into a drumstick. He would do it during recess, right at the bell. I had to run away as fast as I could. As I ran, it occurred to me that I could devote myself to running and running my entire life.

The kind, flighty, scatterbrained teacher didn't have a clue, and the days went by: bite to bite, week to week, drawing to drawing, and I drew myself tiny, beside my father, mother and brother, with a giant eye. An immeasurable tear fell from the bulging oculus. The kind and flighty teacher called my parents in: I was well-behaved, but I didn't have a proper sense of proportions.

Based on her verdict, my parents bought me a workbook to practice.

Draw three lines that divide the sheet of paper into equal parts. Divide the paper into six squares with the same surface area. Make two crosses of the same size that take up half a page. Cut the posterboard into sections of equal size.

Thanks to those notebooks, I learned to enlarge and shrink figures and objects in exact dimensions. Balance and consistency. Rationality and reflection. Structure and equity. Symmetry and breaks.

And a single mantra: everything in fair measure.

NIGHTMARE

I open the door to a bog-standard hotel room.

Number 999.

I insert the card to turn on the light and "La Chica de ayer" by Antonio Vega comes on.

CUTICLES

I bite my nails really bad, until they bleed. Cats, for instance, use their claws to climb, but ours are only good for harboring bacteria; like our belly buttons, armpits, dimples—completely useless. I've been trying to make my fingernails disappear from my hands for years. They hurt. They remind me of a hook, a hoe, a nineteenth-century hanger, a chimney shovel, scrape, scrape, scrape.

Sometimes I insult them:

Stubborn, swampy cuticles!

Since I was diagnosed with depression, fragile fingernails grow under my solid ones and they itch and laugh and corner me and if I let them grow long, I scratch myself at night and leave cuts on my face and chest.

I am the scratch-woman.

Science claims that these are unverbalized emotional deficiencies.

What can I do so that I don't scratch myself? Bite my nails.

Why does my body need long nails? Intractable lesions, asleep or awake, in a trance, focused, in the weeds or on big feather pillows.

How to put an end to this psychosis of biting and scratching? It started very young. As a little girl, I tore off my scabs and stained my sheets with blood. My mother told my father that there was always, always, always blood in my bed. Such a narrow bed for a such sickly little body, so much blood, spotty and dark.

What's wrong with this girl, for God's sake, what is wrong with her?

And she scrubbed hard, rubbed dish soap into the bloodstains and the nasty spot came out, although it left a yellowed trace there, mysterious.

When they signed me up for piano lessons, I started biting my nails even more: mercilessly and with a sense of sadness.

My body is a lost battle. Anyone who has touched me knows this. It's like stroking rusty, stippled walls.

Some of my piano teachers smacked my hands:

Don't leave your hand there! Lift, lift! There's a pause. WHACK!

I remember those slaps as if I'd gotten them yesterday. Bruises fade, but the rap of bony hands does not.

At least you're used to pain.

My hands are not piano-playing hands, they are rusty anvils. One evening, an expert in palmistry—who was that studier of hands? Anyway, a woman with ancestral wisdom told me that my square, thick, flat hands are perfect for pyramid-building. That if I'd been born in Cairo, with golden hair and between the two humps on a camel, my childhood would have been different.

Like, more… distinguished?

Despite being like mosquito zappers, my hands are good for some things: I write with them, use them to reach shelves, unearth a marble, wrap myself in petals, pay for a pepper, wave a sad hello, sign agreements, pull my zipper up, pull it down, rant and rave.

VENLAFAXINE

Is the medication I'm taking for depression. Brand name: Vandral Retard. In me, it causes hyperactivity, nervousness, nausea, dizziness, vitality, the urge to wreck floors, walls, knolls, stoves, washbasins. Yawning. Yearning. Paucity of possibilities. To sum up the combined effects, I'd say it submerges me in a state of wild transcendence.

Like yoga, but at warp-speed.

If I had to compare myself to an object, it would be those little wind-up toys. They're dead, you wind them up, and they come back to life.

I took a usual dose of 75 mg at first, and then they increased me to 150 mg because I still couldn't stay on my feet. I've never felt so embraced, not even as a baby. They hold my hands, arms, crutches, long sleeves and short sleeves and lace T-shirts.

Not even all of those hands were enough.

Now I take a daily dose of 225 mg.

When you're getting used to a pill that affects your brain, you are yourself but with reinforcements. It's like a balm for wounds.

The brain doesn't scar, but thoughts do.

In a way, the point is to not allow those thoughts to crack and fork off toward a dangerous and not-at-all desirable existentialism.

The brain is a landscape. The mind is its ecosystem.

The main problem with depression is that it takes a long time to cure. Months. Years. Lustrums. According to what I've been told, I had a grandmother who suffered from depression her whole life. She died. I never met her. And she still has depression: it hasn't gotten any better because, even in the grave, there are things death cannot defy. How can death overcome depression if it's the most inhospitable, sadistic, repetitious, sticky, tyrannical, immaterial, diabolical disease I've ever had? They haven't come up with an exorcism to eradicate it from the body. Ghosts shrink from it, cannibals eat it, dogs growl at it, gravediggers need it, the feather duster pushes it around, gods fear it. One day, mid-crying fit, I begged my partner to yank that flaming, hurtful substance out of me. I felt it in my chest.

Get it out of me, get this devil out of my body!

There was pressure, a bloated tire, an organic steamroller, steelworks in my lungs.

Get it out!

All they can do is hug you tight. And wait.

I think about my grandmother sometimes. What she had to suffer. How she must have been treated. If she filled a bucket, bathtub, or cistern with fresh tears. If they made a broth out of them. Watered a palm tree. Washed their faces.

How lovely: to wear your grandmother's tears on your face. And take a picture afterward: click.

NIGHTMARE

I'm digging a grave to plant a tooth.

    The next day, cackling and giggles are heard underground.

CAPSULE

I think I know what it is I'm trying to write. The verb is *to encapsulate*, pertaining more to the scientific realm than the humanistic one. I want to encapsulate moments and store them, cryogenically frozen. I tend to keep science at a distance because of its, shall we say, dehumanizing nature. And yet, I must admit there's still an affinity there: I keep a capsule collection too.

I'm not so much a writer as a person who devotes herself to the *encapsulation* of emotional phantoms.

I need a refrigeration system. A 50x microscope and a surgical gown. I need a strongbox where I can deposit my radioactive material. Where no one will touch it. It's fragile now, dying under my desk. When I can't think of a word I give it a kick and spill all the amniotic and cerebrospinal fluid I've been hoarding. I need to be sure some living thing moves inside my capsules. Something impetuous, young, long-living, something that drinks water and stretches its limbs. Yes, those are the moments I'm interested in. The ones on the edge of the precipice. Which precipice? you ask yourselves: there are no precipices in Madrid; in Mallorca, there are cliffs with houses at the edge of the sea.

Once I dreamed that the sea swept away our Mallorcan home, the gargoyle house, and that my parents, intrepid captains, were trumpeting:

Even if it kills us!

They had climbed up the tall tower of my house, which is like a mast, and just like that, my mother threw an anchor down to the street, zero safety precautions, where it struck the bald head of an enormous man carrying a ferocious, purple squid curled on his chest and who complained:

Watch what you're throwing, lady!

The squid was slick-black from another squid's ink, Christmas coal, scorched ash, a pleural spill. I don't know! You can't decode dreams!

I woke up with a liter of saliva in my mouth.

Now that's a shipwreck.

When I was four, I was attracted to dens, wells, hollows, potholes, sinkholes, the pencil sharpener hole, windows that opened into the night, the tunnels we passed through to get to our gargoyle house, which was terribly far away: the edge of the edge.

Books (I just thought of Manolito Gafotas and shuddered) told me about those dark corners I was drawn to. They spoke to me indirectly. Hypnotized me and left me feeling groggy: hungover.

Pharmakon is written as a response to those books that told me things.

As a little girl, it's hard to talk back; you acquiesce:

Yes, sir, whatever you command, sir, of course, sir.

I'm silly and kind of slow, yes, sir.

Now I have a voice and a vote: I have a book and I have revenge.

Enid Blyton has lent me her dazzling writer's fingers and Elvira Lindo her odd little boy and Escobar lent me Doña Jaimita who just peeled potatoes and more potatoes and caravans of potatoes and it's because of them that the damn devil depression cannot defeat me and it is on these characters—good, bad, average—that I concentrate while observing death so near.

Doña Jaimita isn't real, I know that, but death doesn't have physical properties either and, close up, it's still really scary.

No princes or beauties or beasts.

Books are my antibiotic and my democracy.

OUTSIDER

I was born an outsider in a land of Mallorcans. I was raised as an outsider eating food from La Mancha: grilled meats, migas con ajo, pisto with egg, asadillo, stew, chorizo patatero, cured cheese in oil, chistorra, pipirrana, cod tiznao, cocochas, lamb's head, Almagro eggplant, torrijas. The books I enjoyed most were in Spanish. I read sporadically in Catalan.

I dreamed in Spanish. I laughed in Spanish. I preferred that to frit mallorquí, to bullit, to Mallorcan rondalles. I danced funky-style, Spice Girls, flamenco. I rapped, imitated Will Smith, Britney Spears.

I've always found Mallorcan boleros quaint and repetitive. My mother dressed me up as a pagesa farmgirl, in a macrame dress with a wide skirt that hides the hips.

Come on, Almudena, go be a pagesa with the other Mallorcan girls. Girls who were named Aina, Xisca, Margalida, Tonina, Mireia, Laia, Joana, Neus, Empar, Marina, Caterina, Miquela, Catalina, Àgueda. Last names Alemany, Cabrer, Binimelis, Puigròs, Bonet, Puidserver, Serra, Rotger, Terrassa, Ruitort, Porcell.

I was the only Almudena on the island. I think I still am, actually. The only Almudena at school. And at university.

They spoke to me in Mallorquí and I answered in Spanish and that's how I spent half my childhood, speaking two languages that were close but different; two beautiful, competing languages, two overlapping languages, from Latin: the brother and sister-in-law of language.

Her parents are outsiders and, of course, this girl answers in the outsiders' language, but what are we going to do about it?

At four, a girl threatened me:

They're going to send you back to the Peninsula on a leaky boat.

At five, there was a song I really liked in Catalan. It moved me:

Puff era un drac magic que vivia al fons del mar,
però sol s'avurria molt
i sortia a jugar

[…]

Hi havia un nen petit
que se l'estimava molt,
es trobaven a la platja
tot jugant de sol a sol.

[…]

Els dracs viuen per sempre
però els nens es fan grans,
i va conèixer altres llocs
del món que li van agradar tant.
Que una nit molt gris i trista
el nen el va deixar,
i els brams de joia d'aquell drac
es varen acabar.

This song is about the loss of imagination. About the fantastic beings who leave you, never to return. It was crushing. When I wandered through the house whistling, a silkworm squished in my hand, my parents would pause whatever movie they were watching—*Basic Instinct*, for instance—because the sex scenes weren't appropriate for my age. I didn't care. As if seeing a good lay was going to upset me, a sensual uncrossing of legs.

What was really devastating was that Puff the Magic Dragon,

the dragon of my dreams that, when I grew up, would never come back, not in another life, and not in a far-off dimension. Not even if I wished with my eyes closed, fingers crossed, soul at attention, eyelashes raised heavenward.

I cried a lot. One time a man named Esteban came to my house and played the song for me on his guitar. Acoustic. I ran to my room; I was embarrassed to cry over a kids' song. I was twelve, I was a young lady, my period soaked through my clothes and I was in the process of getting used to wearing a bra every day. By that time, I didn't cry—or speak—in front of grown-ups. Months later, Mr. Esteban died.

Outsiders are hard to find in Mallorca. Easier in Palma, maybe, but in a town like Andratx, it's tough. My Mallorcan friends let me hang out with them in exchange for being permitted to toss—or shoot—off some remark with respect to my provenance:

You're a Malloquina, but not purebred.

The purebred thing reminded me of, oh I don't know, bulls or Iberian pigs.

At thirteen—in high school by then—Catalan class was becoming strangely dogmatic. I should probably mind my own business, but Catalan grammar is incomprehensible. Besides, we were studying Catalan and interiorizing Mallorquí and we had a pretty big mess with the article *salat* and the *pronoms febles*. I passed my exams by the skin of my teeth. My answers were correct. In spite of my efforts, one teacher failed me because, as she claimed:

Almudena doesn't show love of the subject, her heart's not in Catalan.

My heart wasn't in math, either. And the teachers didn't get all sentimental and earnest.

When I was a full-blown teenager, I got into *Rock Català*. I listened to Els Pets, Lax'n Busto, Sopa de Cabra, Antònia Font, and later, Manel. I loved them. I had a Discman and played their CDs on max volume while I spun around the patio and leapt and hummed and felt the lyrics as genuine pangs and revolutionary truths: colossal, unprecedented poetry. Before I became a fan and proclaimed true passion for these bands, a Mallorcan girlfriend had warned me:

You'll never feel these songs the way we real Mallorcans do.

OVARIES (I)

At sixteen, doctors operated on an ovarian tumor they had confused with appendicitis, endometriosis, or an enlarged spleen.

It was cancer.

They wished with all their heart for it to be a mistake. A medical error. I was a minor and they had to remove my ovaries. A teenage girl isn't prepared for parts of her body to be removed. She barely even knows what they're for (the parts). The doctors were terrified of a possible peritonitis. I was terrified of being embarrassed. Always embarrassed. Embarrassment everywhere.

No girl thinks about her ovaries before she's sixteen. Inside the ova are...

Other Almudenas. Little Almudenas.

Teeny-tiny. Sick.

My mother was scuffing at a ceramic tile with the toe of her boot and a nurse or someone interrupted her: You can't erase the floor, ma'am.

Cancer. Cancer, they repeated to my parents. Tumor, tumor index, your daughter. The daughter who was fine yesterday and now might not make it until tomorrow. The daughter with a half-smile because... is this girl blatantly smiling? Someone gently explained to me that my body was like a movie theater. And the important thing about a movie theater is... what is it? Come on, Almudena, take that pillow away from your face: the screen, the image quality, the spell, the light, the actors conversing in the twilight. Your big window onto the world.

What I didn't know was that a scar would split me down the middle. I wasn't ready for that division.

I am Almudena, the person on top of the scar: an earthquake.

And Almudena, the one underneath, rhythm and legs: a military march.

STYRON

William Styron, who I'd never heard of, was recommended to me by my old editor, my friend, my great prescriber of interesting fictions, most of them morbid. A guy who calls himself *Alb*. If you want to get along with him, all you have to do is read with abandon, know what's new in literature and be honest. This last one is essential and for the time being (I think) I have managed it. In exchange, I receive valuable feedback, such as *Darkness Visible* on my towering bookshelves. Because in our house books are God and on Christmas Eve a book was born and the Virgin isn't brushing her hair, she's reading. To be concise: our perception revolves around the books that stir us. The planet, our rented orbit, revolves around a book that burns, boils, and remains upright.

Nightwood by Djuna Barnes, for instance.

It was painful to read Stryon during my depression, but I would do it again a thousand times. The action of turning pages so replete with truth soothed me and I sought to identify with him. Because he got better. And I could no longer stand my condition: I wanted to kill it, kill my despicable state with witchcraft, satanic spells, anything. I jibed with Styron in some chapters and in others not at all. What I liked most about his book was what he baptized depression: "despair beyond despair." No better way to interpret it than as the sum of accumulated despair. One despair that becomes another, bigger despair and the despair keeps growing like big families do, or cotton thistle on wild hillsides. It is desperate, depression is, bashing itself into a glass window, and I have discovered that healing consists of containing myself. Ever containing myself. It is nonstop despair impossible to control. The day comes when you want to explode with despair like a firework, period.

Let it all end in glittering pieces.

If only that accumulated despair could be like taking off winter clothes. From the outside in: first the coat, then the scarf, gloves, ear muffs, fleece jacket, thermal socks. If only we could rid ourselves of depression by undressing, shy and slow.

JUNK ROOM

I have a junk room that I climb through. Get inside. Get lost.

If my head could be likened to cramped space, it would be that junk room: small, cornered, dark, hospital lighting. It ends in a point and one day, tucked inside the sleeve of a sweater, there was a cockroach that I had to remove and pick up in disgust.

Mountains of clothes fill the junk room. They come up to my waist: a Himalaya. There's a loose piece of wood of unknown ownership. A dropleaf table. A Tom Hanks movie. Small scratching posts for cats. Frosted mirrors. An oxygen tank. Sandals in sizes 36, 37, 38. Fishnets. A Santa Claus with wide-open arms—HO! HO! HO!—and a package of expired rice. Well, I'll stop. There's a lot of stuff, *a lot*. And I pass over it, stepping and stomping snow, bowed legs stirring the clutter.

I break a pair of goggles.

I have to lunge to reach a shadowy object located in the back of the room. My creased passport, for example, placed inside a cardboard pizza box. Three big steps that crunch on something below: a travel-sized blow dryer? Lint rollers? A bell jingles.

I leap.

Halfway through the expedition, a safety pin sticks me in the knee; sharp, stiff, open and bright, stuck between a picture of my ex-boyfriend and a book on chickenpox. Blood beads and stains a wool hat my mother bought in 2012, for the next winter. I'd forgotten about the tatty old thing.

A sign with a butterfly motif: *¡Bienvenidos! Mi casa es su casa.*

There's a meat cleaver that shines with murderous intent and aims for the palm of my hand. *Psycho*. I have to dodge it. My junk room is a human head in the midst of a crisis and I pick through it the way somebody hunts for a black truffle: carefully, choked up, stifling the sackfuls of tears that stick in my throat.

I'm warned by an ENT: your vocal cords are strained.

I'm examined by an ophthalmologist: I can't test your vision; you have cried a swamp.

A bag of cement blocks me from advancing to the end. Why do I have a cage if I never had a bird? Deep down, one knows it isn't good to keep buried the stuff from one's life, it isn't good. But the stuff is like this because my head is stirred soup. What can I do? It isn't Diogenes syndrome or a lack of space. It's that I don't care about anything. They are idle memories, mashed experiences, mourning days, wedding days, days on which I sighed so often that there's a cocktail glass with greenish-black dioxide still there at the bottom.

One day I had a snail. It lived on the ceiling. I named it Crocanti.

I don't dare go into the junk room alone. Even though it's my property. Lately, I've decided to enter the cave of oblivion with people I trust: my partner, my friend Matilde. On this adventure called life, what I've struggled with most is to be taken seriously. For my words to have permanence. For this to happen, I thought that at some point I would have to grow, grow, grow. Make myself voluminous, as voluminous as men.

Men!

When I was seven and in my bathing suit, I went up to one of the workmen at our house and drolly proclaimed:

I love Butragueño!

My mother was sick of me talking to the workmen. My brother, meanwhile, was attempting to stick his finger in an electrical socket. Why are sockets the size of kids' fingers?

And childhood happened, brussels sprouts happened, the Band-Aids that fell off our ankles and stuck to our white tube socks with stripes at the top, a never-ending schedule punctuated by a varied assortment of curiosities: why is oily cheese so gross, what does it mean to be a virgin? Are nuns happy? Formal words reverberated in my body such as: assets, parliamentary commission, prophylactic, kerosene.

Sometimes on Sundays there were frozen churros and a pleasant puddle at the entrance to my house where we stepped with rubber soles and Velcro:

SPLASHHH.

Grown up and graduated, several months ago I still wasn't taken seriously when I mumbled into the phone:

I don't feel well. I need help. I have this sense that I'm at a party but totally separate at the same time.

Maybe, in order to be taken seriously, you have to go to extremes. As words don't work, or gestures or smoke signals or screams and much less tears or formal discourse.

I didn't choose to be born into this world where, after a gorgeous day, it suddenly rains mud. Rains mud!

What can you do when you mumble something civilized and nobody listens? When you're speaking at a proper volume, nice and slow, easy to understand: mic, please. A loudspeaker, *merci beaucoup*. Well, my last resort was to build a junk room of madness, a mix of overdose and emotions, sweet biscuits and melancholy, glass jars containing a scream, wool and denim and cotton bulimia, a texture of longing, invertebrate pets, roundtrip flights on low cost airlines (Madrid-Palma, Palma-Madrid), the woman next to you praying the rosary, may God forgive her, while you hope to die during take-off or landing or in turbulence and no one suspects your fixation on the abyss, the blackness, the emergency landing in Honolulu and the tragic breaking news.

NIGHTMARE

For some reason, I keep a bag of rocks in the closet. During the night, I wake up munching on the pointiest.

At dawn, I have a broken jaw.

A maxillofacial specialist concludes:

You are suffering from an involuntarily tensing or grinding of the dental structure, with no functional end. As a patient with common bruxism, you are unconscious of the problem, and (if your emotional state remains as it is) you could be at risk of suffering tension caused the adventure of living and the nostalgia that arrives at dusk when you've lost someone or something to death and a pronounced wrinkle between your right cheek and chin, insinuating battles with grief and distress, angst and agitation, queries and whines, waste and whys and a deep, dense lake and an empty house containing only a rug and a neck turned around toward the past with no hope whatsoever of rational approbation, always toward the past, as if seeking... what, as if seeking some phantom, the neck is made for twisting like a screw, given that if you don't note any deficiency in yourself, the most sullen of all deficiencies, it will stalk you viciously, this surreptitious gust of wind that keeps every one of us pinned to the wall (observe the giraffe, the animal that represents the future of the vegetable era).

An abstemious measure would be... Take note, ahem, ahem:

Leave the irrecoverable to one side: the painful pressure comes from inside and it's possible that in less than ten years you will exceed the sensitivity threshold of your periodontal receptors and, as a result, suffer a massive destruction of your facial features (which, by the way, are quite youthful and plump) and irreversible wear and tear on the musculature of a considerable portion of your face. This will seriously impede your ability to smile.

RETWEET

"Could 'sad' be the word with the most synonyms and antonyms?"
    Aroa Moreno Durán @AroaMD

I'm interested in this world of lost birds and winter poems because of death. I'm living a race against time. So as to die well, I groom myself, watch my health, document my life, have fun, exercise, and read Faulkner.

Respect.

When I reach that foul and desiccated place, I want to be in good shape. No cadaverous or scruffy state for me. A toast to death and its invisible authority! What this means is that I make sure to shave. Simply put: death could be the most media-worthy event of my life (everyone will be there, I think, looking at… a coffin? Kitchen floor? Gully? Secondary highway? Bathtub? And at that exact moment I'd like for my image to be both clean and hydrated). Please bear this in mind, whoever reads this: I do not want to die with dirty hair, hairy legs, bruised eyes, split lip, with an insect buzzing around my body, laying eggs near my crotch.

To die well is a poetic act. To die with smooth skin and smelling of fresh-cut roses. That's all I ask.

So death is the intended beneficiary of all my sessions with a razor and aloe vera. All the accidental nicks and cuts and rashes and the massages with healing lotion. Am I in love with death? I might be. In death, there is overpopulation, crowds, lines, waiting lists. People who wait in line for lottery tickets are already well-practiced for the queues they'll encounter in death.

It's confirmed: so much do I owe to that inhuman presence that I don't know how I ever managed to be born. The miracle of birth (yours and mine and other x number of beings) must be connected in some way to an impure, almost divine desire. Here we go! Time to kick and babble, kick and babble!

Birth is a cannon blast.

I shot out but my mother never mentioned that her baby went flying, smashing into the wall, so intense was her desire to live. I swam in her womb; I was born knowing how to swim underwater, a sea urchin tucked in each hand. I've spent some thirty-odd years in this responsible, real-life thing but now a sinister air gathers around me and, when I'm halfway up the stairs, whispers *climb no further*. Not another step. Go down, go down to the dark basements of existence. The advice I'm given is: well then just don't think! This is what my mother urges me: don't think, don't think, don't think, but I'm not thinking, damn it. I'm hearing a voice like radio static, forceful and powerfully persuasive, exclaiming:

Vaporize yourself!

I owe all the exams I ever passed to that voice and it is present in most of my writing. It usurps my personality. It destabilizes me.

Since I was born, my mother has spoken to me in CAPITAL LETTERS and I reply in CAPITAL LETTERS. Our CAPITAL LETTERS are exhausting, an entire childhood and adolescence fraught with CAPITAL LETTERS, always CAPITAL LETTERS, until they lay us to rest or consign us to the grave: sickly, twisted, spindly CAPITAL LETTERS.

In this book, I'm trying to analyze a sick brain. A euphoric brain. An evasive brain. A brain so peppered with memories (with oneirism) that I'd like to grab it, wrench it from my egg-shaped head and stick it in the washing machine with a good dose of Oxiclean. Make it spin. Make it clean. Make it dizzy. Sometimes my head hurts. Not an ordinary ache: it's when I take a leap. Fine, but we don't tend to take a lot of leaps in life and anyway, I'm not about to turn up at a clinic and say *I leap and it hurts my brain*, because if I'm not an Olympic gymnast, then what does it matter.

Does it prevent you from completing your daily tasks?

I ask myself whether healthy brain activity is compatible with the ecstasy of living. Or if the brain isn't made to get aphonic, chattering, drowning in shock and saturated with sentiment. I used to have a lot of respect for the heart as the primary organ. Its ventricles, atria, etc. Starting at grade school, you are taught that the heart (yours and everybody else's, they say) deserves respect and beats and never tires of the boom, boom, boom and thus that organ is king. It's featured in songs, "Listen to Your Heart," by Roxette, "Happens to the Heart," by Leonard Cohen, movies (in *The Gleaners and I*, Agnes Varda visualized a heart-shaped potato and stuck it in her purse), and in famous lines from history, from the well-known *Casablanca*: "Was that cannon fire or the beating of my heart?" and many paragraphs in masterworks of universal literature.

I recall a section from Lawrence Durrell:

"Who invented the human heart, I wonder. Tell me, and then show me the place where he was hanged."

And the book by Carson McCullers: *The Heart is a Lonely Hunter*. The heart: a hanged hunter. Could be a good definition for what we carry inside.

MIRTAZAPINE

Is the name of the second drug I'm on. Brand name, Rexer Flas. My favorite, to tell the truth. When everything goes wrong, when my emotions jam and my mind points only toward the kitchen— the knives in the kitchen—or the bathroom—the razors in the bathroom—I take a Rexer and fall asleep, on pause. I'm inside a TV, suspended. A frozen image of Almudena. I like that: life on pause, STOP, the world keeps spinning while supermarket trucks stock the empty shelves with milk and mushrooms. We should always have that option. The world as a still photograph.

Dr. Magnus told me that it was a gentle antidepressant. I can confirm this. Gentle and marvelous. The venlafaxine works in a less direct way by livening up my nerves, though more efficiently, more incisively: the pill is fire-red.

According to what I've read online, when combined, the two pills I take (Vandral Retard + Rexer Flas), are known as California Rocket Fuel. Rocket fuel. I could go to an international launch site and propel myself into the stratosphere, I'm full of toxic fuel and I function by propulsion, more Martian than Earthling, fist raised in the air. Can't stop me now: three, two, one, go.

My head is becoming cone-shaped, this is true. And my body like a bowling ball. I look pregnant and my ass has never been so big: never ever. I'm scared to look at myself from behind me in case I squash somebody: watch out, I'm on the move. Actually, now I don't even look at myself. This drug, Rexer, is extraordinary but it causes weight gain. My body is not my body from before. It never will be. I feed myself eagerly. I'm constantly hungry. I can down a pear in a second and a half and I crave all sorts of flavors: peanuts in with stew, artichoke and chocolate, red wine and white rice, cilantro and sardines, whatever, I would eat a dry porkchop under the table when nobody's looking and feel fine about it: I've turned into a marauding hyena, half-cannibal, half-person, I settle for a life comprised of eating and sleeping, eating and sleeping, eating and sleeping.

Depression has led me, then, to the beginnings of civilization, to life at its most basic, to hieroglyphs, to kissing a Dilophosaurus and slathering fresh herbs on the soles of my feet, to playing football with my hands. One day, somebody offered me his bus seat:

Here, you're pregnant.

And terror-struck, I sat. Just like I used to sit down at my desk in school. It reminded me of that motion. You never forget sitting in a chair at a school where you are going to be bullied and insulted. Once, my classmates threw a piece of screwed up notebook paper at me. Inside were the boogers of almost every kid in the class: foamy white, green, black, sickly yellow, nose-bleed red. Every time I sat down, I used to check that there wasn't a tack or hardboiled egg on my chair. That gesture alone made them laugh, me checking my chair just in case. But not looking was worse: oh, who knows. I don't know which was worse.

I didn't have time to take stock: I lived to cross off the days.

NIGHTMARE

The scene is a peaceful home. Over a fire, I'm cooking sausages on a skewer. My father sticks his head into the fireplace and, hair alight, asks me if they're too charred.

My fingers are covered in grease and smoke. I tell him they're delicious.

My father had long hair, silky pilgrim-knight hair, curly at the tips, and the sun gifted him almost uneasy natural highlights, pure biotin, spontaneous cascades on his skin, a certain youthful aura... until his kids arrived with their need for fire and sausage, fire and sausage.

Ever since I was diagnosed with "major endogenous depression," time has stopped: I feel a futureless tension. I try to read so as not to lose the habit of linking invisible abstractions. One of the books that has been the best company is an essay by Virginia Woolf, *On Being Ill*, which describes the scant literature exploring illness as its main theme. Its only theme. Obviously, it excludes self-help books and some marvelous metaphorical texts, given that the *Quijote*, in the shadow of each one of its sentences, narrates the evolution of a psychiatric illness. Or Kafka's *Metamorphosis*, a book that—according to Juan Aparicio Belmonte, a writer friend with wending lucidity who was my companion and guide in the Hotel Kafka creative center in Madrid (so charming, Kafka in Kafka that day)—contemplates what would happen if our child had the worst possible disease: the unimaginable worst. Worse than death.

To be clear: if our child was a repellent pest in society's eyes, and his own.

Depression could very well be situated between the adventure-based illness of Alonso Quijano and the familiar ones of Gregor Samsa: right there, balancing on one leg.

Virginia expresses something so relevant and lucid in her essay *On Being Ill* that I must mention it. When Virginia speaks, stop; stop and listen because only a handful of geniuses are born each year and Virginia Woolf is of the most beautiful and neurally vivid minds to have ever yawned on our Human Earth. She argues that illness makes us more perceptive, more spiritual beings. That illness elevates our cerebral sensors and instills itself as a kind of sixth sense in our body, a body we believed to be so well-proportioned, malleable, and known; well, nope. To put it graphically, the body is sex and ignorance. Anyone who suffers a mental illness sees the world through the eyes of a wounded bird. That damage is transformed into kindness is a useless teaching of weak and worn arguments. Whoever gave strength such high standing? No more boxing metaphors, please. Two in the ring, vacuum-sealed steroids. No more men in military dress. Enough fights to the death. I vote for the softness of lamb's wool and Snuggle Bear. Sign me up. Here is a vertiginous quote from my dear, brave Virginia:

"Incomprehensibility has an enormous power over us in illness, more legitimately perhaps than the upright will allow. In health, meaning has encroached upon sound. Our intelligence domineers over our senses. [...] One should not let this gigantic cinema play perpetually to an empty house."

Virginia Woolf defends us, the depressive ill. The time has come for fragility to take the stage. Goodbye macho men and limitless female sacrifice. May softness, slip-ups, feeble anguish appear in our books. Without so many blows that we buckle under them. Without vanity or prideful revenge: crying five big fat tears that lie heavy on our faces, just like when we were kids. May Sisyphus rest, may he relax, may he be squashed by the stone and may he just unwind. Let there be peace. That fault should finally triumph is compassionate justice. Let it be named, let it be heard, let it quiver. Toss the obsession with self-help into the bin and cry, cry, lift the lid off despair. We are losing precious loves along the way. And it hurts like a lightning strike. As a child they taught me that the bolt strikes and after the flash comes the thunder, but what is the bolt? It is depression.

MATURING

I matured poorly. The other girls (and some boys) matured effectively. In other words: if they were in first grade, they matured like a first grader should mature. Or that's how I saw them, anyway. I wasn't infantile, no, not at all; I skipped that phase, I've never been infantile. Strange, how little we respect that term.

Infantile: the best thing you can be when you're 3'2" tall.

I was figurative. A dreamer to the max. Anywhere and everywhere, scattered mind, heart in stories, wetsuits, disobedient in outrage.

I was pursued by a strident voice: Wake up!

Ramshackle
platonic little girl
in the corner at recess

At the close of her workday, a teacher locked our classroom door (I remember that door: thick, brown, striking), leaving me inside. She didn't remember that I hadn't left yet. That I was in there, lost.

My mother arrived at school holding a ham and cheese sandwich for her daughter and couldn't find me. The other kids were there, playing with bottlecaps, end of the school year, start of summer, bare shoulder blades. My mother asked where I was, she couldn't find me, I had dark hair, half-straight half-curly, streaks of uralite, philosophical eyes and a mint green polo shirt. A thin little voice that sounds like it's cracking at the end of each sentence, and a fat ponytail. Because you see, she has a lot of hair and it needs to be pulled back, and when you tell her something she looks at you, kind of slack-jawed, but she isn't stupid, she's just... how should I put it? How can I say it? Fixed in wonder and relatively silent, she tiptoes through the world and is embarrassed on her birthday, she doesn't like her birthday or people telling her how big she's getting (but don't remind her that she's little, either!). She doesn't really enjoy compliments or kisses, she's not very affectionate. A child who plays on her own and sings on the terrace when nobody's watching.

Where is she, for the love of God, where is she?

While my mother interrogated the freed children and their parents in the courtyard, I was still behind a sturdy door. I have a few vague memories, or rather sensations, of that moment. I suppose that I shouted and banged on the door. Scratched at it. Pounded at it. And as usual, thought I was going to die. It was strange to feel unprotected in a place where I was so carefully watched. In the first instant, I calmed down when I saw that I was locked in. For whatever reason, I assumed the teacher (Gema, was that her name?) would sense that something was off. That she would think of me. And though I tried to prolong the heavenly peace of mind that I—foolhardy child—was indispensable to the adults, minutes went by and Gema (?) didn't remember me and I heard the happy shouting of the children on the other side and I started to feel thirsty and hungry and anxious and I sensed chloroform in my throat and a clock hand piercing my hard metal face and a trembling behind my cheeks and I don't know if these are the symptoms, but it's possible that at four or five years old I experienced my first anxiety attack without knowing what anxiety was and if I'm not mistaken (it's hard to rewind!) I was afraid that place would remain silent and at the same time I needed silence because the kids were shrieking outside—a hullabaloo of high notes—and me, from inside:

"I'm here, I'm here!"

You couldn't hear anything. It was horrible. To top it off, the lights were dark and they didn't turn on when I hit the switch and I just couldn't understand it as the lights in the school always worked, and I sensed the end of my life was nigh and simultaneously my brain sought solutions for not staying conscious: there are games in the classroom, go play and forget that you don't matter to anybody, go to sleep on a mat until morning and spit at the teacher with rage the next day and hit her with your inch-long fists and your strength of a country wheat-spike.

An indeterminate amount of time went by. I sat on the floor, defeated and guilty over what was happening to me. Certain I would be scolded, I didn't want to be found, or maybe I did, who knows—a little girl doesn't understand notions of social fairness—and I morally condemned myself for not having left the classroom on time along with my classmates. I cursed my curiosity, my silence, my lack of presence, my timidity. Above all I cursed the timidity that kept me prisoner: herpes stuck to the heart.

How many hours, seconds, minutes, did I have to wait until I heard my mother's voice? I have no idea.

Childhood is the opposite of the passing of time.

My mother approached the door and called:

Almudena? Are you in there?

And I answered with a tear-soaked capital YES. The most miserable affirmation of my first years of life.

I waited there inside little longer while they called the teacher Gema (?), who had the keys, to come and open the door for me. And she came. And she came dissolved in *I'm sorrys* but she didn't touch me, didn't look at me, didn't hug me or put herself in my position. I thought I was going to be scolded. That the scolding was waiting for me at home. What a cruel world: first confined in a lightless room, then exasperation, and more darkness at night. As it happens, I escaped and the telling off went to the teacher, who I remember as a redhead. I noted that my childhood had triumphed for the first time, although it didn't take long for them to categorize me as a brave girl, a poor little thing.

When thirty-three-year-old me remembers myself at three (thirty years ago!), I understand my mother: what can you give a little girl like that? A lollipop, a smack, a whack with a shoe, viscera, a tuning fork, a druggie's needle, a tissue to wipe her boogers, her tears, boogers, tears, boogers, tears, until she turns thirteen and they diagnose her with, I don't know, attention deficit for abnormal development? It was my fault. My mother had me and nursed me, but the blame lies with the baby and her crying.

Through pain and compassion, we learn how to say I'm sorry; we learn be a better person by meeting better people; we learn to pray through obligation; we learn, gradually, how to get used to the cold; but no one teaches a mother how to be. I know all sorts of mothers and mine did what she could: she coached me and issued me with a battery-powered engine.

Go forth, my daughter, go forth.

The fact that the engine has rusted over the years, that it became feral during my adolescence, that there is no fear at the limits of my conscience, or that I was by nature fierce and stubborn and introspective and unbound, was not her responsibility. There's no formula for a person's character formation, it's more a universal mystery, one influenced by all the crushes, the books, the pill bugs, the happy girls, roadrunner boys, marbles, the movies that break your heart and the ones that are too cliché, the summer sun on high, the animals that licked your face and the ones that scared you (I was terrified of pelicans), the inescapable commitments and that planetary power that was stewing in my stomach: rebellion. I needed to let it go and apologize.

Mamá, you are the reflection of a Marina Tsvetaeva line I read on Tuesdays and some Sundays, so as to put myself in your shoes:

"In a such a girl, there are forces even a mother such as this cannot control."

MEMORY

Pound the table
As if that table
Was the mind.
Alba Sabina Pérez

My memory insists on reminding me that I have suffered. That I've been hurt. That I've experienced pain in all its forms: abdominal, physical, climatic. And all three at once: meteoric. Almighty pain. Only God knows that.

I've spoken to God on two occasions. The first at fourteen, when I asked him to grant me the gift of straight hair. I had been spending a lot of time observing a curtain tassel, stroking it. Slowly. A dangling object I admired as the pinnacle of beauty.

God, dear God—I began—all I want, oh soaring God—I implored—all I want is hair like the strands on this tassel.

I started pinning the threads back with clips, combing and pulling them into ponytails. A whole year bewitched by a curtain tassel that swung like a hanged man. I'm not sure exactly when the infatuation ended. Slowly, my hair had become straighter. An almost extraordinary thing. God had bestowed it upon me. I confess that I was also using a straightener. I don't know if it was a religious miracle or an electronic one, a miracle of ions or scalp genetics. No one will ever know. The fact is that God granted my wish. And things started to get better. I'd been convinced that I was shunned at school because of my wavy, frizzy hair. The root of all my problems was capillary. The bullying could be blamed on my unruly hair, on my body, which I covered up with long T-shirts. I got bad grades because my curly bangs were all I could think about. It could have been a coincidence, but all of that ended with the secret plea I made beside a curtain, magical tassel in hand.

Please God, my God, hear me from your galactic throne.

God hearing you once is an absolute honor; twice is too much.

The second time was because I wanted to be a writer. I had no choice but to appeal to God again. I didn't know what to do or how to start. My texts were governed by an ineludible clamor of voices and descriptions of nature. I thought that maybe I could enter municipal writing contests: competitions organized by the town halls of Villatuerta, Fornalutx, Guarromán, Son Sardina. That my name could resound in the pages of local papers. The Nadal and Planeta prizes would come later. I had an inkling, an intuition, and I was right when I repeated to myself that being a writer begins at the bottom: in the grottiest catacombs, at the Earth's core. So I dug. I dug more than I wrote. Dug with dirty hands and a garden spade. They would come later, the sweet scent of success, the fancy fountain pen. The heart-stopping autograph. My book presented on TV: *The author we have ALL been waiting for.*

I would pay homage to my dream library: a whole shelf of Nabokovs and Enid Blytons, full of compliments, exaltations, caresses, imaginary weddings. Ada and Georgina (alias George). Kirrin Island and Humbert Humbert's motels, Uncle Quentin and Van Veen, Aunt Fanny and Cordula de Prey-Tobak. Vladimir Blyton. Enid Nabokov, who cares, they rescued me from the short circuits I suffered as a result of birthdays, etiquette, and the rage breathing down my neck. I married those books in church, at the courthouse, and down the longest hallway in my house. The ceremony was a crowning moment, there being just one witness: a broad-faced cat watching in astonishment.

Blindly digging down into a blank page. Not to plant a seed or bury a dead body. Digging for digging's sake, running into sharp rocks, extraneous paragraphs I didn't know how to end and didn't dare flat out delete. DELETE. Dense roots that demanded experience born of error and stopped me from going deeper into the stories.

Lack of technique, theory, and reading. Worms. Nits. Setbacks. Lack of oxygen, more than anything. Desire requires lots of oxygen and lungs need passion and passion breathes ecstasy and ecstasy feeds delirium and delirium leads to death. Death is a hollow.

Don Quixote and Sancho know. For months I wrote for a tree I could see out my window. A stone pine. It moved with the wind and I wrote along to its sway. Whenever I got stuck, I watched it move, dance, and then my hands moved over the keys. A little more. Letters, words, whatever, a devious exclamation, a rhetorical question, an obsessive *what*.

I don't know if God looks more like a nebulous entity or a pine tree. I do know that my memories of those religious encounters don't give me any pleasure. They were ludicrous prayers. The right to privacy is the right to madness. And I exercised that right, writing and praying. Spells of agonizing solitude (early examples of, I'm sure, self-harm to my brain) with intervals of impotence and self-flagellation, suddenly interrupted by my mother: ALMUDENA! DINNER!

What a way to break the spell. My mother—I say this with love—wielded an axe of reality. A hardware store of disappointment. She started with an axe and went on to acquire a pair of pliers and a large drill.

It's easy to demolish a world. What's difficult is maintaining it.

My mother, drilling into the air of utopic dreams, and me resisting the ridiculous life embodied by her pan-fried steak. I addressed a picture of Carmen Laforet: How did you do it?

I ignored my mother and returned to watching God, who in my mind was a pine tree, closed my eyes (the phantasmagoric can only be conjured in darkness), and attempted to transport myself to another dimension where a wayward girl, a girl with no knowledge or family history or inherited talent or breakfasts in hotels, focuses on generating the desire, more desire, to write something approximating a book.

First, one must load up on strong substances. I'm stirred by signs that cry: APOTHECARY! CHEMICAL SPILL! HAZARDOUS GOODS!

I regularly pierced the backseat of our car with the sharp tip of a compass and nobody noticed. There were times when I didn't write a single sentence. Why bother, if my words weren't brilliant, if they had no effect. I would fill my lungs with buoyant air. Air, purified by a mother's axe. I looked at the swaying pine, at Carmen Laforet, at Enid Blynton and Nabokov and the long-legged spider spinning a web that unraveled every night. The struggle to write is always the same: a slight poetic shudder when confronted with a big chunk of reality steak.

The fact that I wanted to be a writer was cute until I got to be fifteen. Sparks might have flown when I read, but it was time for me to focus.

Find a non-utopian profession, Almudena. A job with a briefcase. Playtime is over: be responsible, study, get good grades. Books are for vacations.

Suddenly, books became secondary, a treat, a prize. Like a traffic accident that cuts you half: before books / after books. Why yes as a little girl and now no? Because I already knew how to read, they said. I already understood the Ten Commandments.

And stories?

Bah, stories are a dime a dozen.

I am both orphaned and not. I had to form a personality during very brief bursts of light. In fleeting, nocturnal episodes. My obligations didn't allow me time me to think. They came in successive waves: innumerable extracurricular activities. Hours and hours in the car. Steam on the back window. Finger-drawings: the whale from *Moby Dick*. I longed to play. I couldn't stand the clickety-clack that carried me from one music class to the next. From tutoring for English to tutoring for Math: in my pocket, my calculator turned on by itself. The batteries wore out.

Again? The batteries again? Now, let's see. If at least you'd been studying... God, such a pain in the neck.

Such exhaustion.

What's more, we were always at the dentist. Way too often. Our teenage years were spent in his office. I've popped pimples in his bathroom mirror. He rebuilt one of my teeth. He filled my brother's mouth with colorful braces. And he plucked out my mother's gingivitis with the flick of a knife. They argued. Her teeth looked like a dog's maw after biting a cat. She hid her mouth behind her hand. She growled, licked herself clean.

Don't look at me, Almudena.

We called him Mr. Carrots, the Dentist.

He charges us just for talking, my mother complained.

We swung between arriving late and not arriving at all. We rested in the gargoyle house, fanning ourselves. In my parents' opinion, the world swindled them, cheated them. Don't trust anybody, ever. And they made photocopies of every piece of paper they got; I regularly came across duplicates of their certificates and receipts in the breadbox, on the lid of the toilet, or strangled in the chandelier. They all started with:

On x of the month of x in the year xxxx, and in the presence of x.

Terrified by the gavel of justice and the judges in their ridiculous curly wigs, I put them on my father's desk.

Papá! I found a paper!

Well, you know what to do: into the document folder it goes. One must anticipate, daughter.

I would rifle through those papers, some folded in disarray: what awaited me in the future. I stirred and stirred and shut the fat folder. A folder impersonating a stomach. My father's belly: full of figures. The elastic's going break, damn it, everything's so fragile these days.

On Fridays, my father wore a tie. Just Friday. This delighted his colleagues. If my father ever earns a place in history, it will be for that: sporting a tie on Fridays.

When I was seven, I admired the women on TV. The men all looked pretty much the same, very similar.

But the women.

There weren't many. Two or three. The ones I observed most closely were the women who reported on the weather. Meteorology. They stood. Elegant and serious. They spoke normally. They didn't have to dance or take part in any embarrassing spectacle. They weren't drooling over a football player. They didn't take their clothes off. They weren't cheering on a bullfighter. They didn't cook. At that moment, they weren't mothers. They weren't advertising laundry detergent or playing a spiteful ex-girlfriend in a soap opera. They were wonderful, the weather girls, my heroines. The whole family paid attention. The news program proceeded with its macabre events and dystopic warnings, but the big meteorological moment always came in which the woman, on foot, demonstrated her power. She was going to tell us whether or not it would rain. Cold or hot. Cloudy or clear. Those women were stating something conclusive and true, a blend of biology and excellent public speaking. Heat waves. We got dressed in the morning according to their advice. If I couldn't be a writer, I wanted to be a weather girl. With a magic wand pointing to the isobars: a storm was approaching, an atmospheric front.

I bowed before them.

CARLA

I have voluntarily started looking after a four-year-old girl. It's a marvel how a damaged childhood can be healed by someone else's happy one.

What scares me most is that her time as a blonde meteorite will break. I carry her on my back like a work of art —I don't know—like an authentic Giacometti figure. Or more than that. There are many works of art and only one Carla: no other shall be born. I carry her in my arms the way I would have wanted to be carried at four. Nice and tight, not thinking about the sore muscles sure to follow, eyes wide and shining, injecting her with life or the desire to live: the taste of summers to come. I care for her like I would care for a mini-me; I put all my hope and sensitivity in her, seas of feeling and understanding for Carla: she is exhausted by the love she receives and I am in ecstasy, childhood trauma repaired.

Inhale, thirty-year-old woman, inhale before the beauty of the world.

I can use the money her parents pay me—they are wonderful with me, that open family—although what they cannot imagine is how much Carla heals me, more than all the drugs that course through my veins. I tell Dr. Magnus that Carla is so healing precisely because she isn't my daughter, because her upbringing doesn't depend on me, only her little wild animal pleasure. We've walked barefoot and stepped on rocks. I have helped her pee behind a graffitied wall. She has climbed trees and told me that she stores her dreams and nightmares on one of the branches; she's really scared of witches but we both know they live in thatched huts in Paris-France. We've danced to whimsical songs in the cinema and I've pushed her in a shopping cart at top speeds down slippery supermarket aisles. We took our picture in a photobooth as we made Maleficent faces. She has eaten my boring grown-up ice cream and I have eaten her colorful kid kind. She has given me drawings brimming with flowers, glitter, bristling wolves, new grass, hot air balloons and a single sentence:

When we are sick, our heart sounds like a drum.

Some evenings, after a frenetically good time in the park, the sun restless on our bodies and a smile so red it seems about to pop, I give her a calm bubble bath with a plastic whisk, an iridescent cup and all her toys.

Some float and others sink: a metaphor for existence.

She makes me milkshakes of eggplant and cream and butterfly wing. Bubbles spill over the edge of the tub. She relaxes, though never completely. Carla is child who plays with air. Once, I saw her stop in the middle of the sidewalk and let her hair, her curls, sway to rhythm of the breeze.

Instead of thoughts, in her head there is a running river.

My deepest desire is for that river, dragging her toward the difficult years of growing up, to flow into a tranquil basin of compassion and sense of humor. As for me, I would never go back: so unanchored was I that I sucked on the wrapping paper covering my new birthday books. Nobody saw me. Nobody cared. Then I read those books greedily, the gift wrap dissolving in my stomach because I'd unwittingly swallowed it. The books were all I had. I was scared because I had ingested wrapping paper. I was eight and I was scared of death. Nobody saw, nobody cared. Except the inhabitants of my book.

Did books save my life?

I think they did: absolutely. Turning the pages, I felt like dying was impossible, even though I'd eaten gift wrap. I was reading and couldn't help becoming other characters. They distanced me from the girl I was.

During every relaxing, madcap bath I give her, the ones in which there's so much splashing it stops my watch, I wash Carla's hair and massage her head. Her head hurts after squeezing everything she can out of life and for a moment she is still, eyes closed, as I draw circles over her temples, and she thanks me and observes: You know what? The brain has boo-boos.

And I intuit that she knows about my depression. How? What magic powers do children possess? Can she read my mind? Did she install a hidden camera by the couch in Mr. Magnus' office? Wonders never cease. She brings out the shine in life: she opens her eyes, laughs through wet lashes, splashes me with warm water that also feels cold, and concludes her poetic address with a masterly offer: Want me to make you a strawberry shake? With chair leg and avocado? Extra foam.

I say yes, of course, yes I want those milkshakes, all of them disgusting and undrinkable. For the first time, I understand childhood as a pleasure and not a punishment. As a kind of intelligence that only lasts a certain amount of time. Highly radioactive material for demanding adults. It isn't fair to touch or to change or to manipulate it: that treasure doesn't belong to us unless it is from afar, from *our thin red line*, from the stunned armchair in which we sit. The conclusiveness of this paragraph strikes me and saddens me a bit, while I take pleasure in the fact that Carla, wounded by intensity, continues her awesome journey through parks and joy.

STEPHEN

Julia Stephen was Virginia Woolf's mother.

A methodical woman, strict with the blood pressure cuff and her tidy, neatly pressed white smock, she spent her life in hospitals where the gravely ill convalesce, begging for help to come quick: an intestine of voices.

She was an excellent nurse. And she had narrative urges. She was raised among writers and philosophers who frequented her home. Her uncle was a politician. She was a fierce defender of agnosticism. She posed as a model and pre-Raphaelite painters captured her on their canvases. Her arm at a right angle. Blurry hair. Crooked raspberry smile. Naked, I don't know.

She wrote in her notebook: "The ordinary relations between the sick and the well are far easier and pleasanter than between the well and the well." The notebook is an essay titled: *Notes from the Sickroom*. She wrote it for scholarly purposes and with a single dream: though she had no shining diploma to frame and display in a handsome case, she had learned to intuit what was wrong with a person when they felt this or that. She did not have a nursing degree and she wasn't a writer. She died fast. She couldn't even take care of her daughter Virginia during her adolescent years.

Julia Stephen, what was she?

Wise, altruistic, half mother.

She was a helper, nothing more. She was obsessed with the breadcrumbs that got into the patients' beds. She viewed that sad nuisance as one of humanity's great ills, capable of ending someone's life. Itchy arsenic between the sheets. In the gloom, she sought solutions:

"A very good way of avoiding these is to pin the lower sheet firmly down on the mattress with nursery pins."

"Crumbs lurk in each tiny fold or frill."

"[…] crumbs are banished […] temporarily, because they return again with every meal, and for this the nurse must make up her mind."

Breadcrumbs: sisters of depression. Julia Stephen mentions, discovers, a barely visible evil, yet one which contains a truth. The invasion of crumbs in clean sheets. Depression is made from those crumbs (baked thoughts, frosted flour, flaming leaven) which itch, stick, multiply, return, and provoke intermittent tears.

"The origin of most things has been decided on, but the origin of crumbs in bed has never excited sufficient attention among the scientific world, though it is a problem which has tormented many a weary sufferer."

This point—lyrical and intelligent—gives meaning to the word *care*. If only Julia Stephen had published a whole book on breadcrumbs and their inexorable return. It would serve as guide for artistic creation or an index of the philosophy of transparency. To understand someone as Julia Stephen did: to recognize its invisible ills and calmly pick them up with clean hands; one by one.

NIGHTMARE

Two worms are conversing:

    Worm #1: Have you ever been inside a liver?

    Worm #2: No. Have you?

    Worm #1: Yes.

    Worm #2: So, what's in there?

    Worm #1: Words.

PUSSY WILLOW

If there was one thing I liked about school, it was dictation. I loved transcribing. I didn't have to think, language sprouted on its own. It thrilled me to write fast and finish before anybody else, without a single spelling mistake, and challenge the teacher:

So, now what?

It was gratifying to write without knowing what would come next. I'm drawn to things done unconsciously, almost stalely. The panacea for my time at school was concentrated in those moments of tension: unfinished stories, dictations done in parts (my first lesson, perhaps, in writing with gaps), having to wait for the next sentence and the imaginative commotion that it produced.

Perennial fuzz floats through my brain.

The teachers dictated adult stories. One day we had to transcribe a paragraph from *One Hundred Years of Solitude*. It was, for me, an outpouring of pleasure. I became feverish. My pen ran out of ink. I made my *L*s big and round. I crossed out a sentence in order to go back and write it again perfectly, I underlined the word *ice* and noticed that my classmate next to me had spelled it wrong. We lived in Andratx, a town with two supermarkets.

What was this beauty by this Márquez person? Where in our small school were my teachers hiding aesthetic ambiguity? These were not the same moral tales we were taught in our textbooks: fables of the dog that talked to the rabbit about not eating all the carrots in the garden and saving some for his family. Kindness. Responsibility. Doing the right thing. The dictations were grander words: they were closer to literature. And I was there, oozing happiness with a spent pen, keeping quiet about how much I liked that composition of language.

So-and-so Márquez.

Sunlight filtered through the window, a single shaft flickered through the blinds and one of my classmates pretended to catch it in his hands.

Sunbeams are the film directors of childhood.

I think it was wintertime when, for the first and last time, I was kicked out of class. And it was during one of those dictations. The Spanish Language teacher was something of a dreamer, somewhat religious and very reflective, and he would gaze out at a bird in the distance, roll up the sleeves of his striped shirts and always checked to make sure his shoelaces were correctly tied.

The word PUSSY WILLOW appeared in the dictation. I wasn't stupid. I was ten years old and more or less knew its meaning. Vaguely. Furry nubbins. Stalks of small, silky mounds, soft and wild. Still, I wanted to ask what PUSSY WILLOW meant. I raised my hand. Laughter—the murmur of laughter, how sweet it is at first—began to fill the room and half the class lost focus and the teacher didn't want to answer my question and I asked again about the word PUSSY WILLOW because what was the problem anyway? I was simply flirting with a concept that combined nature and sex.

The teacher, having checked that his laces were tied, forbade me from continuing with the dictation and sent me out of the classroom and into the hall for being funny. I wasn't funny, I swear. I never even tried, I was always scared nobody would laugh. How awful, the funny people who are the only ones laughing at themselves.

I was of two minds. I was most bothered about knowing what came next in that dictation, that guy Márquez's story. And I had to swallow a 2.8 grade that really upset my father. Ever since, the word PUSSY WILLOW is there like a sign of vital rebellion, a linguistic impulse. I learned that when it comes to provocation, the more abstract and sincere it is, the better. And I learned the power of language when it has a bit of an echo.

RETWEET

"I'm going to take a pill, before life starts to have an effect."
   (Elena Figueres, *in memorium*)
   David Trías. @DavidTrias

VHS

In the beginning, the gargoyle house in Mallorca was small. My parents made it bigger over time and turned it into a chalet. They gave it status. The house grew, better-fed than my brother and I. We were well-fed, but the house always got more. Cement, plaster, mud, silicone, I know those smells well.

I'm allergic to my own childhood.

There's a VHS tape that disturbs me. I've seen it ten times or so, looking for a convincing—though elusive—explanation. My brother and I grew up in the midst of renovations. There was always a renovation underway somewhere near us, and we had to play away from the work being done. A shriek:

Almudena! Don't you go near the workmen!

For a month, the workmen and I were good friends. They talked to me about football, Maradona, Guardiola. And I would approach them to see what was happening. They drew flowers on the bricks, with my name in the middle. My brother and I changed patios, moved our inventions workshop, bug laboratory, fight ring, stuffed animal school, bike course, etc., depending on what work was being done at the time: a glass-enclosed terrace with oscillating umbrellas. A landscaped parking area. One bathroom less. A dormer. A cupula. Rustic stairs to improve the view. A sewing room and another for musical instruments. A stellar chickencoop. A palatial skylight.

My father had an old-school video camera that, to see what was being filmed, you had to fit your eye to a tube. My brother and I playing in the area. In the video, you hear our voices, our footsteps, our shouts. There's an occasional glimpse of us, like two hummingbirds whizzing by a perilous windshield. We are not in focus for even a full two minutes. The video is of the house, with my brother and I in the background.

The ghosts are the children.

The video is about an hour long. An hour of kitchen, landing, office, bedrooms, and verandas. My brother and I always as secondary characters, imagination as our flag and a resin of loneliness on our skin.

There's nothing wrong with taking a video of rooms. Recording the dead air of a concrete moment in time. In the video, there's a moment when shining specks of dust appear, flying sequins. They float. And a simultaneous peal of laughter and a wail from my brother. He was like that: he laughed and cried, ate and slept, looked at you while closing his eyes, pulled out a blade of grass and planted a coconut tree: that's my brother.

What frightens me is to hear my childhood without seeing it. The shadow of the renovations. My parents' fascination with brick and manganese. Their pride in making a room bigger, their satisfaction with the places they designed themselves; memory has several coats of paint. My mother's painting of a hunchbacked woman still hangs askew in the hallway and my grandparents take up an entire wall: they were photographed down in the mouth. In the paintings, my grandmother doesn't cry. Her photographs are happier than she was.

My brother and I exist more as adults than as children.

HOSTAL SINATRA

Life continues to stimulate me, but
Not erotically like before. In the past I saw
The sea and wanted to make love to it.
Theodor Kallifatides

One day when I didn't want to be seen crying, a day that was
scandalously bright and I could conceal myself behind a hat and
a huge pair of sunglasses, a day when I felt that the burden other
people bore was greater than my own (there are days when I'm
not a writer, but a trucker transporting butane and cowbells), I
went to a hostel near the Castellana in Madrid.

I walked the whole way there (I had no strength to catch a
cab, or a bus, but I had the strength for unchecked walking). I
got lost and cried like a six-year-old. All I needed was a cool bed
and a pillow to hug. Any pillow. The elongated structure that
saved me from sharp-edged nights after a shitty day of school
bullying. Memory foam. The one thing that provided relief from
the sorry, brutal echo of the teachers and students who made fun
of my lapses and floods—emotional, cultural, artistic, creative,
contemplative—and, after their quip, tittered behind a cham-
pagne-soaked mustache. Polyester. Who pointed out that my
handwriting was "like a booger." Cotton. Who compared me to
an obedient dog, "woof, woof, woof." White. Who told me to
shut my trap, since I could bore "even the dead." Orphanhood.

That hostel—let's call it Sinatra, Hostal Sinatra—was
equipped with a small, broken television and a fan that turned
and shot desert sandstone directly at the humble, single-pillowed
bed. I wrote this in the Notes app on my phone:

Days go by, some good, some bad, most of them acceptable. My body moves through the hours with enough solidity, but my mind doesn't manage. Something doesn't fly within me, and consequently, not next to the world, either. My brain's shadow is stronger than its light; icy cold clogs my head. I live in the Arctic. The northern part of the Arctic.

My tears are falling icebergs. From this height, they hurt, those tears, which are merely frozen childhood. I've turned into a stop sign, a woman who barely feels like a woman, or a living being, nothing, since nothing makes me feel alive or passionate or dreamy or feverish either, nothing puts an impulsive flush on my cheeks. I've been waiting for these crises to pass. I've been patient. And I think I've tried. Generosity for generosity's sake has been really healing. Involuntary laughter. Affection in my cat's little squinted eyes. Days away from home, in Budapest and El Médano. My aunt's hands, her touch, her hugs, her food. The way she sews: her needles radiate love.

There are beautiful sights on this planet, I can't deny that.

Over a year ago, I perked up a bit when my partner showed me some silver birds planing through dark black clouds in the sky. There are liters of sensorial experience on this planet. There are good people. There is poetry in checkered tablecloths. There are kids who run and pull me along with them and give me great big slobbery, candy-stained kisses. In spite of everything, in spite of seeing it and feeling it, it hasn't been enough for me to say: I want to remain here, walking.

My feet have hurt ever since I was little. When I walk, I mean. Shoes hurt me, all of them: they rub, blisters spring from other blisters. Maybe I wasn't meant to walk in a hurry. One night, I roamed the streets with a piece of metal and smashed up some paving stones. Sprained hip. But that's another story.

The pain today is worse. And I really, truly feel it. A tightness in my chest, a wheeze that comes and goes, practically howling,

expels, inhales, collects and stores traumatic air. Inside my will
to live, there is an office. An emotional bureaucracy. A ruined ID.
The impossibility of drinking in the world the way someone drinks
a glass of wine: mindlessly and with appropriate composure.

It might be the closest I've been to writing a suicide note.

The hostel cost me twenty-seven euros.

My personality was forged in a solitary pool. I will never get sick of swimming underwater. I can hold my breath for almost four minutes. My life consists of swimming underwater wherever I step, deep, subterranean, until I encounter the shark; that is my terrain. I'm looking to get burned.

Even on nights when it thunderstorms: I'm underwater.

In the book *Notes on Suicide*, Simon Critchley underscores that a fair share of suicide notes should be considered extremely high literature. Though it's hard to see them as such. His entire essay disrupts, propagates, shouts its head off, superimposes itself, thinking through end-of-life notes and why we have a hard time understanding them as literature's loudest outburst. If they actually are. If they were written with the last breath: the ink of farewell. Why aren't more books published containing the suicide notes of artists? Five or six tomes. You can count them on one hand. A press: Suicide Editions, LLC. So many writers, painters, film directors suffered from depression, madness, schizophrenia, OCD, abyssal vertigo, death wishes, or got involved with a cult that incited them to dress in purest white and roam the forests looking for lost souls. If suicide notes happen, there's no reason to hide them. They are what we have left: the crumpled paper behind the void.

If a person I loved left a suicide note for me on their nightstand, I would analyze it grammatically, word by word, until I squeezed out all its juice. I would perfume it with the scent that transmitted their loss. I would keep it inside a music box that played, oh I don't know, Nick Cave's "Into My Arms" or "The Blower's Daughter" by Damien Rice. I would translate it into Latin in case it clarified something for me about its original roots. I would translate it into French, which is an elegant language.

DISRUPTION

I fall. I don't know where I'm hurt on my body. I double over.
My muscles creak and my joints stiffen. I writhe. I don't know
where I'm hurt. I stretch. I break my elbow. I shudder. I choke.
I don't know where I am injured. I discover my head is twisted
around. Now I have eyes in my back. And neck. My shoulder is
dislocated. I don't know where I'm hurt. I try to compose myself.
I roll over. I can't get up. The lower part of my ankles ache. My
pinkie. My thumb. I'm experiencing a disturbance. I need to call
someone, urgently. A stretcher. I have to reach someone. I try
to get to my phone, dragging the hard bone of my coccyx and I
notice that my pupil has slid far over to the right, far to the right,
my pupil hurts, my iris, eyelash number twenty. I keep crawling,
dislocated shoulder working as pickaxe. I'm ruining the wood
floors, expensive wood floors in an apartment that isn't mine. I
crack the parquet, nailing it with my bone, I'll have to confess,
report my madness, I will suffer an attack of shame and rage
and poverty. Poverty, too, a modern feeling, a contemporary
sentiment.

I reach the phone and, with the intact part of my ulna—
broad and armored—, call emergency services, say that again,
what's wrong, we don't have much time, you're not the only person in the world with an emergency, of course we don't work the
whole day, what's wrong, if you don't know where you're hurt,
you need to look, look for the wound and when you find it call us
back with something more concrete, more specific please, we're
not here for chitchat or grandiose speeches or poetic pranks, this
isn't a Top 40 Hits call-in or afterhours confessions, but we are
at your disposal. I hang up. I hear a beep, I'm alone again, ulna
slotted between two pieces of parquet, I stretch in an attempt to
get my muscles, my bones, my lungs back in place: deformed

creatures are not welcome, they simply aren't, Quasimodo and Frankenstein come to mind, and well-formed creatures aren't welcome either, but what does that matter, what does it matter when I'm living and I explode into tears because I don't know where on my body I am hurt, even though I look for it, invoke it, imagine it.

With a clear throat and the purity that precedes honesty and an opening little cough, I curl up into spherical ball and cry out: God, carry me off on your crystalline sleds of Christianity, because I just don't know.

JERUSALEM

In a hospital in Jerusalem, there is a psych ward reserved for people who believe they are Jesus Christ. The lunatic wing. I learned this by chance while watching a show, and I thought it was a fabulous literary and psychological phenomenon, how the Bible and hard reality converge. How literature is knotted to life, to the brain alterations to which we are subjected: always as salvation because a person, young or old, looks at the stars there in the distance, all those brilliant points of light that appear and disappear and burn out and have form but are simultaneously immeasurable, untouchable, inexplicable, gorgeous, and doesn't know what to say.

What?

I imagine the Jesus Christs (male or female; there are women, too) in the hospital in Jerusalem talking amongst themselves, doing what we normally do under capitalism, but in a hospital ward: competing to be more Jesus Christ than everybody else. Envying the Jesus Christ next door. Tripping them. Rending their tunic. Growing out their beards (in the women's case, their pubic hair), bragging about new miracles—more experimental, more aesthetic—like impregnating a single man with fatherly ambitions. Turning a pig into a fly. The rain into caresses. The sun into a starving rose. A sloppy boy into a girl of Messianic purity, tongue blue from so much sucking on lollipops. Perhaps the Jesus Christs attempt to escape life's uphill climb in this way: believing themselves to be figures from literature. Believing that they are better, miraculous beings.

So they steal white sheets from hotels and wrap them around their heads or wear them as a gown. In short: garb themselves appropriately. Then they head out onto the biblical scene and wander, lose themselves, walk and walk until nobody can find them. Some are discovered numb and dehydrated, moaning Jesus Christ's name while others are trying to heal a bloody scratch with the power of revelations. One, specifically, suffered tendonitis of the neck because he did nothing but watch the clouds all the time and declare unabashedly, without qualms, that he was able to make them move. The clouds were obeying his thoughts.

We've all fallen. They aren't crazy. The mind is youthful and gets stuck in the books we fell in love with: a prophet in the Bible, Pinocchio and his screws, Anacleto, a Secret Agent and his eternal cigarette, Gregor Samsa on his back, desperately kicking his legs in the air, Don Quixote deluded and sane and normal and congested and beaten, Lucette plunging into the sea between two turbid waves; Susan, Neville, Jinny, Percival, and Bernard handling bread shavings and calling them "people," Chip and Dale naked in a barrel, Alice in the cities and another Alice in Wonderland, Bianca Castafiore singing to a parrot, Guybrush Threepwood with a pot on this head, Celia and the Revolution. And it's okay to be masters of this fleeting encounter, for a while, out there in the Holy City.

BLAH BLAH BLAH

I wrote my previous book, *The Acoustics of Igloos*, at a wobbly table. I felt in concert with the piece of furniture: trots and gallops following each consolatory word. For the beautiful hands of a brave woman, I wrote a space-masturbation scene and I would write it again a thousand times. It was one of the most triumphant moments of my life. I don't think I'll ever write anything so inappropriate again. The table kept still during the masturbating.

What is writing without a bum-legged table? It was my teacher: that damaged table. To write and hobble is everything.

I never bothered to put a crumpled napkin under the short leg. I enjoyed the discomfort of the words and the inconstancy of the table in equal measure. It was like a table at a bar: flimsy, occupied by gloomy drunks, showing me the flaws in my writing, given that the reader can always be further aroused and I myself was never satisfied: the thrill is invariably far-removed from the words. More often than not, it's in the silences and as I started filling blank pages with words and words and more words, I found I was frigid, dejected at the risk of going off the rails and my words sounding like blah blah blah. It happens to most books. I go into a used bookshop and in the background all I hear is: blah blah blah, blah blah blah. That's my struggle as a writer: the struggle against the blah blah blah.

I don't write at a wobbly table anymore. It was too precarious and too musical. I was writing on horseback and fancied myself a bucolic cowgirl.

There are no teachers. There are people who bravely show their wounds.

I've always been terrified of suffering from schizophrenia. Since I was very young. Since I was eleven. Excessive imagination has that double dimension to it: you might actually believe it. At night, when I couldn't sleep, I would think incessantly of stories and imagine a hobo watching me from the corner of the room. Dionisio Rituerta? He wore a hat with brown diamonds and was one those wise beggars who gives you a spiel and reinvigorates your mind. The indomitable Dionisio Rituerta. In the end, I so believed in him that I actually saw him. Almost spoke with him. Fell in love and hated him and killed him and buried him behind a dead almond tree. Dionisio Rituerta? Can you bury a creation that originates in subjective nocturnal visions? Yes, maybe I did see him. Maybe it was true. He was a man, a master, a creator of wobbly tables. Who knows. I think, though I have no formal diagnosis, only the power of my disturbed mind, that upon reaching adolescence, I suffered from schizophrenia for three straight hours.

I got bigger nipples and schizophrenia.

My mind is like a television set with a broken antenna. The picture turns fuzzy and grey. You change the channel and again the grey screen takes center stage. Alternating streaks of grey. You turn off the TV and the screen goes back and that is even worse and you run and you swallow a Rexer Flas because you can't take it anymore and the drug, thank God, saves you for a while, a few hours during which time you usually have nightmares but at least they are no longer in real life.

Nightmares, if they happen at night and in bed, are bearable. What's unbearable is for them to occur in the world of our five senses.

How strong we are in dreams.

INJECTION

Depression is a plot twist towards pain. I live with a withered brain and what Dr. Magnus did ("prescribing is an art," he declared the other day) is populate it with oceans, bougainvillea, volcanoes, swallows, protozoa: make it chemically livable. I liked his declaration; I'd never considered the art to be found in a psychiatric prescription. A cerebral Big Bang. Starting from zero. Switch on the light. Unbeknownst to us we are being filled with chemistry. Life is chemistry and feeling. On the one hand, what you feel. On the other, what you take in order to keep on feeling.

It's not like I was a sheet of ice, but I had put the world aside. Pushed and swept into a corner, forgotten under the sofa. So as not to see even an inch of it. So as not to come across it and there was just me and sadness, me and sadness: a corset of sadness fitted to my whole face. And pallor.

And the lack of will to even speak my own name.

Almude. I stopped there. I couldn't even manage say the whole thing.

I've applied chemistry to my hair. Chemistry on my skull. Chemistry on my femur and my neck. Blonde chemistry. Chemistry on my eyelashes. Chemistry on my nails. I've dyed my hair so as to be a chemical woman. I was advised to go lie out in the sun like an immoveable stone. And let myself brown. I let the light enter through the strands of my hair and the map drawn on my knee. Sweating inside a red coat under the yellow waves. That was me, on a bench, lethargic and drugged, observing the iridescent green shell of a scarab beetle. One should entrust her gaze to simple creatures. When I got shots as a little girl, I used to concentrate on focusing my gaze so I wouldn't pass out. I looked for a horizon: a dirty floor tile, the button on the practitioner's shirt. A nurse got distracted and he accidentally jabbed me hard with the needle and that's why I have a very round, deep scar on my arm. It looks like an anthill. One day, shiny black ants will emerge and travel over my body.

An injection of light. I did it for months and months: to reconcile myself to the light, to allow it to possess me (if you let it, it turns you into a sphinx), to absorb me until, gradually, I sense the invisible monster, the horrible monster, the shadow-eater, pathological and taciturn, evaporate.

Exorcism by light. I'm blonde now if I get a look at myself: platinum blonde.

SCHULZ

They taught me the adjective *sad* at school in passing, between the rising sun and the one that intensifies at midday. I learned it, never delving deeper into its content, its semantic field, or significance. All words were the same. I had to swallow my spit and pronounce them out loud: *tabernacle*, *filthy*, *diopter*. You wouldn't catch me saying them twice.

It's the immediacy that wreaks havoc.

When you're a little girl, everything seems to come at once: the vowels, growth spurts, losing a tooth, an itchy sweater, multiplication tables, your family on your father's side, on your mother's, the step from diaper to WC, solids, liquids, affection, jealousy, fear, salt and pepper. They will come to know you by your facial expressions, by your attitude toward discipline, by the silly things you do to shake the adults out of their boredom, by your ability to soften in bed and stiffen against the freezing bath water.

Charles M. Schulz invented the mortally depressed child: Charlie Brown.

Experts are waiting to learn whether a child is a vulnerable creature, the possible victim of sadness. Yes, some affirm; no, say others and life vanishes, brushing past us costumed in the metaphysics of the grotesque. The toilet paper runs out as a cloud disintegrates, never regaining that elephant shape we glimpsed one night as kids: never, never. You have to drag out the end of things. There is no cure.

I have trouble writing Schulz the same way I have trouble writing Nietzsche. As a teenager, I used this witticism to hook up with an older guy who I liked a little. I liked his smell. The smell of an older man, gentleman's cologne, yessir: aftershave? Pollinated wheat? Mikado stick?

He had a car, he was twenty-seven, I was sixteen. He smelled of home fragrance, crushed fresh daisies and lemonade, he tutored me in math and the scent clung to the pages of tiny grey squares, aggressive numerals, exact solutions. That numerical stiffness dissipated in three seconds, along with his smell: citrus sweet.

I used to sniff my math notebook.

I carried the notebook with me everywhere. Once I sniffed it in Catechism, Blessed Lord. And I yelled to my parents that of course I was doing my math homework, when really I was sniffing my older adult man, so old it was scary.

The equations and I drugged ourselves on *eau de* man-in-a-suit.

Charlie Brown is a misfit cartoon. Wiggly line for a smile. Two hairs at the back of this neck. A tangle on his forehead. Baby face. Eyes that just don't know where to settle: two birds? And a serious disorientation of whys. Why is he there, why do things turn out badly for him, why isn't he more attractive, why does he have a dog who lives a happy life when he can't even sleep at night? We all know that dog: Snoopy. He's funny, cute, and blasé.

But Charlie Brown.

A depressed kid can't be appealing. And yet, Schulz vindicated him. He vindicated him for fifty years. He was in love with that sad-mouthed, bewildered Charlie who woke up in the middle of the night with questions about death. His boredom led him to think, never to play, and if he went ice-skating, he was the first to fall. He never got cuts. Never blood. Never vampires. Never monsters. Never the news. Never rape.

Comic strip sadness starring a child whose leading role was gradually usurped by a sweet and lazy dog.

The miracle is that he's now in fashion and featured on several pajama sets in Women's Secret.

Charlie Brown, we sleep with you and a brown paper bag on our head.

RETWEET

"Poetry is a noradreline uptake inhibitor and a neurotonic agent."
    La_poesía_es@poesia_es_Bot

TO PLUCK

I spent my childhood summers in my mother's village: it's in La Mancha and called Porzuna. The whole village smells like fresh meat and old sweater. There are four bars, a churro place that's always open, even on New Year's Eve and Holy Days of Obligation, and a park with swings that move on their own. There's a dance club nobody goes to, but which usually opens on the weekends and has retained its 1980s charm. There's an elderly man with a pacemaker sitting in his doorway who tells you a joke, the only one his damn Alzheimer's permits:

Who is the *pato*'s wife?

La pata.

Who is the *cerdo*'s wife?

La cerda.

Who is the *caco*'s wife?

La caca.

And he explodes in laughter.

The village is like any other village affected by what they call Empty Spain. Twenty years ago, there was happiness in these streets, children's races and cheap balloons, even bubbles floating freely and popping with glee near a streetlight in the plaza. Garlands. String lights. Folklore. A makeshift stand where some guy named Feliciano Brusconte sold firecrackers.

In that happy time, when I was five years old, I plucked a chicken. They killed her in the courtyard of my grandparents' house, cut off her head with the slashing of knives, and she started running around ruffled and in circles and she hit the wall with hooked claws, flapping her wings until her final breath. She lasted a few minutes without a head (without a brain?) and went stiff shortly after. The entire courtyard filled with blood and guts and veins and arteries, and red blood cells and feathers and clots and the beak dragged over there and I don't know what else, a crest or something: the head (God, I remember it winking at me or maybe I hallucinated it) rested in an empty flowerpot like a plant or a Viking trophy or something. Somebody please explain this to me.

Hours later, it was my job to pluck it. Slowly. With my short, stubby five-year-old's fingers. Feather by feather. The chicken, still whole, lay in a blue wash basin with water (that I do remember) and I was pulling out the feathers with a feeling of unusual awe. I wasn't even wearing gloves. I had to tug a bit on the feathers because they resisted, clinging on to the chicken's corpse, and so each feather was a mystery, coming away with a sort of *crrrek*.

In a way, I was already familiarizing myself with death, right? Feather by feather until absolute, naked exposure.

The final feather would be conclusive: to pluck or not to pluck? I yanked and the chicken gave a robotic shudder, as if she'd just felt life's last pinch: some memory of the essence of having once belonged to this planet teeming with beauty and terror. And we ate her. Every bite was philosophical; the chicken and I had shared moments of intimacy and strangeness and all I did was obey. Pluck, chew, swallow, digest. The chicken tasted good, although I also sensed something transcendental arising from beyond the bounds of the meat. Aside from the nutritional aspect, I was assailed by concepts.

My parents and aunts and uncles drank. They don't know how often I've watched them. Watching is the best way to learn. Keep quiet and watch the human species. Noise is learned outside: after we are born. One learns to protest that which harms your dignity, to defend your battered dignity, constantly, and protect your earthly emotions: everything that has breached your body and left you worse for wear. The unsayable, the simultaneously unhappy and happy: the profoundly private message, the craziness of those days, it made sense, the times I had to bite my fist to stay silent because they were touching (touching? groping!) my invisible part, the part that can't be named or safeguarded, that impenetrable substance, not inside or outside but all around, which is formed when we're born and never rinses out. It's sticky, it needs a lawyer, and it smells like dead chicken.

GRAVE

The year I was depressed, I visited my grandmother's grave in Porzuna. More precisely, I was taken to visit it. The depressed person is a rag doll: they bring you, bear you, carry you up, take you down, they prescribe you milligrams and you spend twenty-fours mute, a musk stain on the short-sleeved T-shirt you wear despite it being winter.

We got to my grandmother's gravesite at midday; a radiant sun lay over her. I don't know what it is with cemeteries, but they gather so much dust that the bushes grow frenzied. The dead are wild beings; they rest on their backs atop the deepest roots of the earth.

Three of us visited my grandmother that day: my godmother—another Almudena I'm honored to share a name with—, my mother, and me as an unavoidable, gluey condiment.

It was high time you met your grandmother, one of them said. I don't know which.

First we cleared away the stones, the pinecones and the pigeon poop that had dried between the letters of her name: A N A S T A S I A. Airborne debris. After the tidying, I tried to communicate with her mentally, with my deceased grandmother, but then angry bees started to sting our feet, our fragile toes exposed in sandals, our defenseless ankles, and I think it was my mother who shouted: The bees are coming!

Turns out, that my grandmother's grave is ringed by beehives. They protect her and not even God can get near my grandmother. She is inviolable.

I was wearing full-length sweatpants and managed to avoid some of the world's most frenzied stings. My mother and godmother were stung a handful of times by three or four fat bees. And that was my brief experience with my grandmother, an experience I'd hoped would be mystical, intimate, reflexive.

The cemetery was deserted and we were sweating and my aunt and mother were hollering in pain in the 100 degree heat, hopping and puffing through pursed lips, heading for the cemetery entrance where a man (part-nurse, part-cop) pulled a bottle of water from his isothermal backpack and splashed their feet, my mother's and my godmother's, with freezing cold water, and I watched as the motion was repeated at least ten times: sprays and sprays of water and ice chips on their feet.

Frenzy within the stillness.

My grandmother is the queen bee.

EPIGENETICS

There is a theory that sounds far-fetched in principle but should be kept in mind, especially if we compare it to the cockamamie things that happen on Earth (toucans with heaters in their beak, identical twins with the same fingerprints, an app to communicate with your cat via meows, holograms that perform live concerts). The theory is poetic, merciful, a consolation, a university study; for safekeeping in a chest in some out of the way place, in the event of extinction. The theory consists of this possibility: children inherit trauma from their parents; of a parent's trauma being so profound that the mother passes it on to the baby in her womb. Trauma arriving by way of a detour. Though present in the offspring's genetics, this trauma doesn't necessarily show up in the genetic code as such: it's a less a scientific fact than a psychological, behavioral, impalpable one.

Trauma as secondary supply.

I know a music buff who wanted to pass his musical fervor on to the baby he was going to have with his wife. He put headphones on his wife's belly. He combined classical music with the Beatles and, I don't know, a little of everything, even Iron Maiden and Nirvana. Every day, the woman's belly grew and grew, accompanied by the headphones that slipped off, fell down, in spite of the ungainly custom-made belt the husband designed. He could not imagine a future son who didn't share his inherited passion.

Fetuses hear voices and TV commercials and the street outside and the crackling fire, the obsessions and insults, the *baaa* of a sheep and a soldier's command, TEN-HUT. They hear even what they don't want to. We are born having heard.

I'm not the only one who, from an early age, has had something wrong with them and doesn't know what it is. I devote my writing to summing up in fifty-thousand-and-one ways what happens to a human heart at dusk, why all this nostalgia and rain and poison when I'm riding my stationary bike and stop at the edge of a cliff to fathom why we jump or are flung in the shape of a volcanic cloud and what there is beyond this dull floor that groans but doesn't give out under our feet after a day at a uniformed job. I write for a heart that bawls more than it beats, a heart that, at the age of ninety, at the bottom of a ditch, will still have a birthday wish to make, since virtue lies in having, at a ripe old age, some desire to blow in the direction of a cheesecake.

And should that come to pass, you'd better hope you can still hear the applause, the fanfare over having arrived—so stalwart and so broken—at this moment, at this magnificent cheesecake and its flaming candles (beware, cakes are inherited too) with fifteen contractures and the wrinkle like a roaring creek stocked with fish and barracudas and floating algae that proclaims that I am still alive, still clinging to the same old story.

What's wrong with us without us knowing what is wrong and there's me holed up behind a book that masks my whole face.

BEYOND THE TEARS

It's not just depression, I tell Dr. Magnus, it goes well beyond the tears. There's no psychotropic drug that can give me back the explosion of childhood.

I'm trying to jump back into the past. Pull the diving board out of my chest and make a little funeral for the quivering wood that has given me so much. Inside, we are no more than a refrigerator ensuring that nothing rots. Not rotting is my chief mission and is why I have baggy circles under my eyes and why I dig my heels in, demanding compensation. How can I explain it? Fill me with perfumed petals and medication. With space stories and distilled magic.

The thing is, I lack juiciness. The fruit inside: freshness. The rocking. The splash. The exclamations. The high-pitched howl. Colors. The pastel-blue sky close at my back. The simple songs, the hop, the skip, the wiggle, the not being hungry because sometimes it's good to forget that our lives depend on breaded pork. And a laugh track and an out-of-focus music video, sugar in the pockets, cracked teeth, antiseptic on the elbow.

I was agitated the first time I went to Dr. Magnus' office. I had never seen a psychiatrist. I met a female one at a hippy wedding, but she wasn't practicing psychiatry there, she was having a good time like everybody else, dancing and drinking and cheering Long live the happy couple!

I'd never gone to a psychiatrist or talked to anybody with a degree who listens to problems. My Aunt Antonina went with me then and she goes with me now, waiting outside the room and reading magazines in the dark. Just because. Not because there aren't lamps or sunlight or anything like that. She sits there in the gloom. Sometimes I think she does it in fellowship with my darkness. And I go into the next room which is small, cozy and austere, a whole couch just for me: a couch of pain, my pain, other people's. The first time, I made myself talk about whatever, since this is the deal: an expressive contribution is required. I didn't know how to act and I've got a tendency to pretend I'm okay and my face pulls a smile even though I don't feel like it. I'm just like the waitresses passing out free canapés. You know, the ones with the super-white teeth. What was that slogan? Ah, yes: "*Sonrisa Profident.*" I'm so old-fashioned. I smile according to protocol.

As regards my first session with Dr. Magnus: I think I managed to fake that I wasn't so bad. My nails were half-painted, my hair was clean and pulled back, eyes dry, and I told him that, well, I was barely sleeping, not eating much, I felt outside of myself (I even saw myself in the third person) and the fucked up situation for young people today, our shitty generation, the shittiness of job insecurity, the shittiness of working for free, the sky-high rent I had to pay, as if I were living in Silicon Valley and not in a neighborhood that smells of fish scraps because the garbage trucks are on strike and when I leave my apartment building I'm faced with SPLIFF POWER graffitied on the wall across the street and a malnourished dog that's been looking for its owner for ten days and, dangling from the powerline, a dirty lace thong with a picture of Dumbo on the front, all of which make me question whether there is a future beyond this desolation.

STRATEGIES

Nothing is working. I looked online for one of those electrical shock devices. To wake myself up. Give myself a shock, a spark. Reanimate the dead arms I've been dragging around day after day. I don't consider any physical pain to be unbearable. I say this, but I haven't ever given birth. Maybe that is total pain.

When I feel bad, I imagine getting shot in my sternum. And, well. I'm curious, even, about how I would feel with a bullet inside my body. Other days, I pray someone will set off a bomb wherever am. The department store, the metro, the dry cleaner, my closet. I don't want them to kill other people, of course. Really and truly, I don't, I swear, but a bomb is quick: BOOM.

Yet it's cars that really fascinate me, cars and their fury of headlights and tight-fitting tires. I want to put myself in front of those machines. I want them to hit me. Without braking. There's something movie-esque about being sent flying and rolling into an empty field. I know what I am saying is crazy. This is why I'm shut away inside my house. I know this paragraph shouldn't be published. I know I'm not doing anybody any good by writing it. I know I write it blindfolded. I know it's worthy of getting pitched off a roof. Still, I leave it written because with depression, you think it all the time.

Ways to kill yourself. Strategies. Your mind ruminates over how to annihilate yourself. I try not to think. I watch TV and don't care what. A game show, soap opera, origami, Wheel of Fortune, desultory commercials, even talk shows. Good God, strike them from the TV guide. Put the hosts in prison. They won't recommend my books, they'll cry that they're rubbish, I don't give a flying fudgesicle. Put on whatever you want.

Princess Di, George Clooney, what else? Don't care. I see them on screen and I'm dazzled by their irresistible force, their quick movements and the sparkle in their eyes. I do three crucial things to heal: don't think, keep still, and swallow pills.

And lately, I've incorporated another activity: I paint flowerpots.

NIGHTMARE

I sit down to breakfast. The coffee is ready. When I go to pour it into my cup, blood comes out instead.

It bubbles and stays hot.

In the brief essay "Modern Melancholy," Roger Bartra considers the nicknames we're given depression: how long will we keep debating, keep changing how we refer to formidable, stubborn sadness? Why can't we settle on a stable moniker for this ill? I saw the little book on a New Books table reserved for Philosophy-Mysticism and I bought it with money I'd set aside for a beer at home, dopey and content, watching a silly romantic movie. By then I was managing to achieve fog-headed half-hour intervals: a big accomplishment. Months earlier, I could only stare at a wall that tugged at me like a magnet and drew me in to beat my head against it. I associated them: wall / headbangs, headbangs / wall. An unbreakable binomial. Over time our relationship cooled, though I still have the sense that walls, biomes, subsoil, beams, pillars and gates, could awaken in me a centuries-old aggression. And so I pretend not to see them, which is how I also behave with certain people: as if they didn't occupy a particular space.

Depression is an obstacle course. The problem is when you see those obstacles with the clarity of a monocle. Life is accentuated in its pain and takes on classist undertones: you are a slave to the illness. There is a master, a lord, the guilt that keeps in you chains. I often think about those comic-strip convicts with iron balls around their ankles. A ball and chain: depression consists of dragging that ball around until—from wear and tear, from apathy, from not resisting the clatter of time—it eventually disappears.

In living, we have to push and pull, like when we open doors. We can't push or pull other people, who would be hurt by those hostile moves. People aren't entrances, they aren't exits. We pull the door and pull ourselves: pull, push, push, pull, and think about which doors are kind. They glide open. Maybe that's where peace resides. In opening and closing doors ourselves: by our own hand, textual words, without intermediaries, alone and somewhat uncertain, with the compassionate musculature of adulthood.

The following terms have been used to diagnose depression: funeral aureus, black bile, black river, invincible inertia, desert island, brain fractures before an irrational world, catastrophic after-effects of love, twilight-induced metaphysical disease, cloudiness of dark humors, an atrocious waste of emotional energy, extreme displeasure, dark saturnine glow, semi funereal solemnity, black explosion in spirit, the terrible weight of an excess of meaning. For Winston Churchill, also a depression sufferer, it was his "black dog." A dog he hadn't bought or adopted, and which pursued him through the halls. A flea-ridden mutt. Churchill both had and did not have a pet. A very close friend of Abraham Lincoln, William Herndon, remarked that "his melancholy dripped from him as he walked." It's true, it's like we are drenched in oil. A kind of walking croquette, dipped in egg, dredged in flour, but not yet fried: sopping and viscous.

My grandmother suffered an attack of melancholy. Eighty years later, her granddaughter suffers from depression. She went from convalescent spa to convalescent spa, from baby to baby; I go from couch to couch, book to book. We both play Snakes and Ladders, but my dice are medical advances and the normalization of mental health, and so they bring me more luck.

Seven children and a miscarriage: my grandmother had a neighbor lady, a friend called La Medarda, who looked after the grown children (there were three or four by then) while she birthed babies. In a small and dingy room, La Medarda entertained the kids with puppets. My grandmother birthed and birthed and her depression grew entangled with umbilical cords and cries of pain (doesn't the time come when there's a merging of

our various pains and we no longer know exactly what hurts?):
so much blood, such a ridiculous name—La Medarda—such
glimmers of somber animality in such a small room.

RETWEET

"You live / letting yourself go / You have ceded so much terrain
/ that you don't feel yourself."
    Rafael Cadenas. @digopalabratxt

RETWEET

"Sometimes you don't feel like doing anything."

"That includes everything else. Whatever isn't anything. Whatever is everything."

"Ugh, that's tough."

Ana Ruiz Echauri. @anaruize

FLOWERPOTS

Living in between anxiety and apathy has driven me to flowerpot decorating.

I can't even classify what I do as an act of painting. Painting is art, and what I do is a superficial craft. This is how it happened: sick of watching tv all day, every day, I got off the couch, my legs responded (the Vandral Retard + Rexer Flas, the Rocket Fuel, had begun to take effect) and bought some ceramic flowerpots at the Chinese-owned bazaar on the corner.

Four or five pots. Some tempura paints. Some stickers. I start painting: pot after pot. On some, I paint triangles; on others, circles or crazy stripes. And doing this, I feel like an artist. I think: actually, I'm not bad at this. I could do this. Until retirement.

Almudena Sánchez, flowerpot decorator, follow me on Instagram.

I work mechanically, the morning goes by and expands into frenetic sunshine. My partner watches me from his desk with a look of never-quite-defined pity and writes, he writes, a future book of literary essays, he writes and focuses on his keyboard so as not to look at me. I paint happy triangles: blue, green, blue, green, etc. And a yellow stipe, then a white one, and TA-DA! Suddenly, a star. I get excited and turn around, run through half the house to tell him:

I thought I'd do a star.

I see, he replies.

I feel gale-force rage that he isn't fascinated by what I'm doing. That he no longer speaks to me with any enthusiasm. At home, I feel like (please forgive me) a mental retard. He cooks for me and watches to make sure I finish my fish even if it takes three hours. Three hours to eat a piece of fish. Three hours with the hake, munch munch. I cry after every bite because it seems an affront that the fish has bones:

Fish are so gross, I say. They all have bones.

An excellent idea occurs to me: I will choke on one of them. Situate it at the back of my throat. I poke around my plate looking for the thickest, least-swallowable bone. And then I contemplate it, analyze it with care. Even if I don't dare stick it far back, I hold it a while in my mouth and it pricks my gum: I bleed and dream, ramble and rave, imagining my death by choking.

Depression isn't the only thing that stalks incessantly; life does, too. That is our great fortune. In my cathartic state as artisan-potter, I feel I'm between the two. Life and death on either side and me, the third wheel. Sometimes I'm more on one side than the other. It depends on the day, the strength of the medication, and the state of the world.

The news is really hard for a depressed person. It tramples me. Not a morning goes by that I don't wake up and think: I want to wear a raincoat inside. One of those see-through ones. To cover me. As if depression drifted through the house, radioactive. I need protection. An embrace. I don't want to bother anybody; I don't want to talk to anyone. Talk about what? Of a sickly sadness? My friends used to want to be with me. For me to make them laugh. For them to make me laugh. Depression should be operable, it should have a remedy: hypnosis, surgery, laser, UV light, eastern medicine.

Fine, I'm sick of this. I submit to the electric chair. I need calm. Touch. Anesthesia. I need it to be that when I describe, oh I don't know, a forest, the sea, birdsong. I don't get a forest-as-a-treacherous-place, where owls twist their heads 360 degrees on their bodies and there I am, rail-thin, brittle, scared, slipping on a mound of cold moss. That when I think about birds,

I don't see them as creatures that shit on my head and caw and are insufferable. This leads me to expound upon the number of bird stores that went bankrupt during the economic crisis and the crisis is an interminable piece of shit that's been around since 2008. More than ten years of crisis. And I imagine the sea—the sea!—and it's full of tourists and greasy sunscreen and the beaches aren't what they used to be; sunburned pale people sporting Rottweiler tattoos and a glans piercing.

Swimming there grosses me out!

This is what I tell Dr. Magnus. Maybe not those exact words, but very close. That worldview. And I think I tell him that I paint flowerpots. He, good professional that he is, restrains himself because I pay him. But I don't want to make my friends suffer.

I — see — nothing — but — misery.

I have suffered the lament of death.

Depression is death's lament.

And I don't know what to do, what to say, what to think: I paint flowerpots.

NIGHTMARE

I'm walking down the street with a group of people. It's a glorious day. My foot gets stuck in a sewer grate. I can't get it out.

The others keep walking, chatting away.

OVARIES (II)

How easily embarrassed are you, on a scale of one to ten?

Twenty thousand.

In my case, shyness is stronger than pain.

A teenager believes her vagina is a singular place, intimate, inviolable, to be kept out of direct light, incredibly sacred.

Four doctor-heads studied what I had so covered up.

Unceremoniously.

Twenty thousand on the embarrassment scale.

They inserted a catheter into my bladder and the bag was clear and heavy and was maybe, even including the post-ops, my greatest pain.

I couldn't pee for a month and half. My stomach bloated. They inserted the catheter. They took it out it. I thought I would never pee again. They wouldn't let me leave the hospital until I did. In the event that I ever managed to pee, I was ordered not to flush the toilet. They needed to see it. They would check. They would approve.

I finally did pee, one day. It was strange. Astonishing. Pee. They all came to see, the nurses, a man strolling the halls, my parents, a friend from school who wasn't that close a friend, the anesthesiologist, a kid holding a dinosaur and a nurse who sang *baby you can't drive my car*.

The removal of my ovaries was divided in three phases: one operation to remove the tumor and a piece of the left ovary. Another, to remove the rest of the left ovary since they couldn't be sure they'd gotten the whole tumor. That was the worst. They used an epidural to immobilize me from the waist down. It was surreal, to be alive and only feel my arms. I filled my head with music. There was infected tissue. And a third operation to remove the right ovary. With it, they took—in passing, and just in case—my Fallopian tubes, and left a developing uterus alone in my body, floating under the weight of the world. Back then, I didn't even know what the uterus looked like, its geometric, organic shape, or why they called it a receptacle. And they left six scars. The biggest, right on the bikini line. They opened me up three times in same spot. The other incisions, less noticeable but almost as irritating as the main one, were made around my belly button and look like teeny tiny lizard bites.

The good news was that I still had *the receptacle*.

That word appeared in my life and metamorphosed many times under various names: life vessel, crucial cavity, fetal container, inside pocket.

You have what you need to have, I was repeatedly told.

Your uterus makes you a woman.

The operations came one after another, over six months. In between, I was kept cloistered in waiting rooms. My parents were the ones who spoke to the doctors. I didn't enter their offices, I was seventeen. I strained to hear, but never managed to catch more than snippets of conversation.

Cancer is discussed in whispers.

Across from my seat sat elderly women fanning themselves. They were highly critical of me: this girl, so young and lush, what has she done, for God's sake. So young and so wild. I felt more judged than ever and started to shout on the inside: howls, ricocheting howls.

I was raised polite in livid silence.

I thought about standing up and popping off my first youthful screed:

Ladies, they have removed a dangerous lump and two organs whose function is still a mystery to me. Ladies, have some compassion and shut your mouths. Ladies, I need to fan myself like you and die for a minute, if that means getting some peace.

Die from living and not feel so jaded.

I have never felt my own age. I've been blowing out candles decade after decade and all for what? I've been as old as a megaphone and as modern as a hologram. I walked the fine line between those two extremes, hopping between the most gelatinous swamps and the cleanest swimming pools and it's really made me go haywire, talking about cancer when in my eyes a perceptive, incendiary childhood still crackled.

I loved not belonging to the conventional world.

To the world of adults.

DIARY OF A BED

Although I wasn't on social media during the most aggressive stage of my illness, I did connect in order to read what strangers wrote. To look at pictures in which I would recognize myself, read tweets in which I would find a pocket of myself. I was stirred by one post in particular.

It was on a girl's timeline. I've looked for it. I don't know her name. Her username. Who cares. She took pictures of her bed, every morning. Her bed when she got up. And she celebrated it on Twitter: I got out of bed today. The unmade bed. She posted a picture of her bed every day. A ritual. A tiny-diminutive-great triumph: getting out of bed. If some Friday or Monday in August there was no picture of her bed on her timeline, it was because she hadn't managed to get up.

Or because she had killed herself.

The force of gravity is harsher on depressed people. Every movement weighs eighty pounds. I don't know, the sky, like, scowls or something, aggressive, threatening, pointing a finger at you. And let's not forget: your commitments are piling up and your relatives watch you with dilated pupils. They exclaim:

But how will you ever catch up on all your responsibilities? Your list of emails and the half-written book and the classes you were going to teach?

What day, what classes, what book—you can't even buy an apple at the grocery store. And if you do buy it, you buy the wrong one, the one with a worm. Your hours contain additional hours inside of them. If you find a sock with a hole in it, (right there on the toe) you cry until you pass out. And you do pass out. And their expectations of you hurt: the joy they're sure you'll feel when you get over this bad patch. Joy frightens you: it's a giant bat. You can't visualize it. They try to help. They give you a little push with their fingertips and you fall over, decimated. Pats on the back are received like hard slaps. The summer is piercing. Who gave the sun a knife? One midday, I went out and came home five minutes later, disheveled, pulse racing, lungs tired.

Running.

It's just… it's just so bright.

I didn't cry, I sobbed. Sobbed until I was dehydrated. Sitting down for a drink at a bar was a prison sentence. You don't want to, you don't enjoy it, your blood stings, your ductus arteriosus stiffen and you hang on, despite the effort it requires—unimaginable, unprecedented, overwhelming. You will rally. You use the visor on your hat to conceal the wrinkles on your forehead. It's a matter of time. Let's not be dramatic. And you spit out a piece of bacon without anybody seeing. Your beer warms in its pock-marked glass. They give you a flower. And you don't see the flower, but its skeleton. How it will dry out: one leaf after another and another until the stem is a rigid stick.

We dry out. Dim. Lose our scent.

Depression makes you a photographer of the majority of the objects you've had some relationship with. It's hard to believe that they exist and serve some purpose. That they have ever belonged to you. A coat rack. You are especially surprised that, at some point, you liked them, you bought them, you assigned them a place and they had emotional value: human enthusiasm.

The toothbrush, such whiteness.

DAVID

Mental disorders stalk me, pitchforks in hand. And I'm prone to falling into their pit of victims. All I do is evade them: if I'm walking strangely in the street, it's because they are pursuing me, pushing me toward their secret chamber. I dodge charity solicitors and mental illness.

Day after day, I see a multitudinous chorus of psychiatric disorders dance around me: I am their bonfire of the vanities. They mock me through the shower steam, sink their fangs into my springy towel, live inside the cream of zucchini soup I eat for dinner. I am enveloped by myriad disorders: panic, obsessive-compulsive, post-traumatic, acrophobic, agoraphobic, Mickey Mouse Stockholm syndrome, dyslexia, selective mutism, Borderline Personality, kleptomania, psychosomatic, hypersomnia.

I find it incongruous, suffering only from depression. On these sunny mornings when my mood shifts—because I adore luminosity, I adore it—I have discarded the possibility that I'm bipolar. I go from the bed to shouting, shouting back to the bed.

Stendhal Syndrome transected by sadness.

A man was dozing in Florence's Accademia Gallery. He opened and closed his eyes so as to contemplate the polished body of Michelangelo's *David*. There is a bench to sit on. He wore a wilted flower in his shirt pocket and was quiet, lost in thought, happy to have *David*'s thighs so nearby and all for him, hypnotic curves, marble eroticism. After half an hour, when the visitors began to clear the room and the lights blinked their farewells, I heard him draw a sharp breath. He unbuttoned his shirt, his chest was tearing up. He doubled over.

He died right there, curled in a ball.
Heart attack.

WASHING MACHINE

We live with a half-broken washing machine. I'll be precise: it works fine. It's just unstable and a little worn down. And old. Tired. It spins, it turns on and off, it completes the wash cycle. It just leaves the clothes really wet. So, when I take out a T-shirt, I really have to wring it well to release all the water's it absorbed. Then I hang it up outside on the terrace—we also have a terrace—because the clothes drip, drip, drip. It's ten in the morning. Well, it'll drip until six p.m.

My jeans are the biggest cry-babies. My scarves. My bras weep like there's no tomorrow and the underwire springs loose. Small rivulets form on the tile: our cat avoids them.

It's not that I suddenly want to write about an appliance. The thing is—having studied the objective correlative in literature, toured the small space of my home (today I managed to take out the trash), paced the living room, tortured myself in the hallway, watched the ceiling in the hope of an instantaneous solution for my anxious, despondent, insomniac state while I color mandalas—I realized that the washing machine has caught my depression. That I smell like depression. It's a strong smell, like farms, like bleach. I smell like a farm on the outskirts of Extremadura or Wisconsin and like cheap Spanish bleach. Look, I don't know how to define it. I lack orientation and a mop. Mental illness smells like distance. That has to be it. People keep away because we smell.

And so I shouted in the living room:
ENOOOOOOOUUUUUGH!

I don't want to leave behind a trail of depression. I sense it, like a wake. Like I have a tail, like a shooting star, a vestige, but a wicked one. Depression pursues and I evade. That's our day-to-day. She catches me, grabs me, and I push forward like an equilateral animal. A game of tag to the death.

Depression is death's tail. I'd never thought about death as having a tail. Horns, sure, but not a tail. Well, now we know one more fact about that unpleasant creature. Death here, death there, death in Strasbourg and in my rickety soul. Yesterday, I knelt before the washing machine and begged forgiveness, crying for what seemed like ages. I hung up the wet clothes and we cried in general: socks, underwear, the whole terrace and me. And in the event that rattle-trap piece of junk could understand me, I begged it for a little help, a little help against this immense depression that is devouring me, swallowing me whole. I clung to a wet undershirt. I hadn't cried like that in a while, so out in the open and not caring at all. Streams of water from the shirt mingled with my tears. The intertwined droplets pattered on the red tile. A puddle formed. The undershirt had a little bow, and I clung to it. Tight. Burning. Benevolent bow. I sat in the puddle. We cried to our hearts' content. The neighbors cried. The windowpanes.

It rained all day.

It was summer.

PHARMACY

Among the challenges generated by depression is the issue of pharmacists accepting your prescription. Hello, look at me, so young, so apparently earnest and transparent. I need you to give me this box of super-strong antidepressants to keep me going. See you tomorrow. See you the next day. They pull a grim face: what could possibly have happened to you, you're in the prime of your life, the age when you should be conceiving plump, healthy babies, if I could go back in time to those years of splendid youth, you wouldn't find me walking into a pharmacy. Not even for cough syrup.

Have you tried passionflower? If it's nothing more than a couple bad days, it'll relax you.

Or yoga! Reiki, group meditation.

How to convince all of humanity that it's not just two bad days. Not even days: they are infinities. And they aren't bad: they are Dantesque. The kind when every effort twists you in knots and one of the biggest efforts is how to explain what is happening inside of you. I try to control my body: don't allow it to head into danger. Because it wanders off. And I'm not the one guiding it: it has become independent and barbarous. At every turn. Every baker. Every relative. Every hairdresser. Every writer. Every person riding by on a tricycle. Look, I can't even explain. Don't make me describe this nonsense under my skin or I will kneel right here right now and start praying out loud. Please.

The threat that I might start to pray gives them an immediate fright. People take religion seriously, who knew? I'm not a believer but I often talk to God, just to talk to somebody. Isn't this by now a schizophrenia taught in schools? Welcome to schizo-religious education. Back to what I was saying: once, I had to show my ID in the pharmacy. They looked at my name, the prescription, my name, the prescription, my name. After a minute came: Well, it appears that all is in order. A minute and two seconds later: Nonononono! Look! It's expired! Expired, I say! Given this discrepancy, I cannot supply you with Vandral Retard.

So, I clarify:

Oh, huh, see, I go to the psychiatrist every two months and he gave me this prescription in case I ever ran out of my medication. They don't recommend you suddenly stop taking it, but I suppose you already know that.

It says it right here: June 6th. And we're well into September.

Yeah, I know, that's exactly it: the summer. The psychiatrist goes on vacation in the summer and I try to as well, you know, go on vacation.

Yes, but the thing is, this drug... you know? You're not asking for ibuprofen.

Obviously not.

Whether or not they give me the Vandral Retard is immaterial. A random fact. What upsets me are the obstacles. The having to fight. The breaching of invisible barriers that, I guess, were supposed to be in my favor: pharmacies, come to me. As a depressed person, I've had to fight twice as hard as a non-depressed person. There are pharmacists of all ideological stripes: the liberal ones who don't even care about the prescription, they don't even ask. Is it for a friend? You're having another bout of sadness and you don't want to go to a psychiatrist? Self-harm, do you?

Then there are the pharmacists who resist at first, but then see the teardrop on my cheek (I live with a permanent teardrop on my face; I've scrubbed with an exfoliating sponge and it won't go away) and reluctantly buckle and hold onto the box until you tug it away. And they give you a bag. Bags cost five cents, they say, but don't worry, my treat, you can't walk around with this, can't have everybody seeing it.

And pharmacists who say no, no, a thousand times no: my second parents.

I drew a map of pharmacies in a notebook. Along the route, I highlight my chances of getting the medication: The yeses, the maybes, the nevers.

BEYOND DEATH

It turns out that Carla, the girl I babysit, is a poet-athlete. She moves between cartwheels and poetry. Her arc of interaction. First, she stretches her legs and does a split and then delivers some poetic observation. She does a back bend and astonishes me with her declarations:

I'm going to be the first woman to play the piano on the moon, did you know that?

She notices everything. And I let her. I also let her be disappointed. And I let her have a good cry when she likes, how she likes, as long as she likes. I let her yell. And laugh and be serious. Eat French fries with her hands or *Frozen* mittens. Crawl on the floor and submerge herself in the grass and the sand at the park and the swimming pool. And in the movie theater.

And in the world.

In short: I don't get between her and reality. When I'm with her, I'm not a grown up. I can't be. I've never known that certainty. The other day, we saw a dead bird. She alerted the friends she was playing with. Most of them went over and circled around it. It was a dead pigeon. Many of the parents present stopped their kids from going near the disgusting thing: It's a flying rat, a disease-carrier. And dead, to boot.

The pigeon lay intact on the ground. It hadn't been run over and it didn't appear to have smashed into a closed window. The feathers shone. The beak and claws.

It soon grew dark and Carla's friends went home. She returned to the dead pigeon.

Let's stay a little bit longer, she said.

She poked at the bird with a stick. I recommended she leave it be; she could look at it as long as she liked, but it wasn't going to move. It was dead. Finished. Lifeless. She asked me if being dead meant the same as not being able to move. I told her yes, in part: not able to move. Or speak. Or be anything. Or just be. She was quiet then, observing the bird. Instead of moving it, she started to stroke the bird with the stick. We stood there for three minutes like that. In silence. She stroked the dead pigeon with a stick and I remembered a scene from *The Hours* in which Virginia Woolf lies down beside a bird while the maids bellow: *Virginia! Virginia!* as they pulled her out her trance. After some fifteen caresses, Carla tossed the stick onto the sidewalk and looked up at me:

Should we kill it a little more?

So it really looks dead. So people know it's dead. It's important for them to know it's dead, in case they step on it or something.

I didn't let her kill it more. We went home. And on the way I thought about the duplicate death Carla was suggesting. Double death. It's not enough to be dead; you also have to look the part. I thought, too, about how much that notion had to do with my depression. I was extra dead, my grandmother died in excess, depression is death's daughter, it's dying twice and fake it five hundred times. The first relief I got, the first break, while sick with depression was when Dr. Magnus certified that I suffered from a depressive disorder. The very words pierce deep and oxygenate you like an epidural in active labor. He was a doctor and he had confirmed it. He stamped my hand, like at the dance clubs. Who could deny it to me now? I could finally exercise my right to be sad. To not smile at the audience. To, most importantly, not see the audience. I was finally going to live on my couch. My lack of appetite, my reedy voice, the swallowing that hurt as if I were scoffing down a shipwreck survivor were all justified. Unlimitedly free. Now I could get out of putting on my chunky tough girl boots, shirk getting up and showering with cold water then hot, cold and hot again. Of behaving like a normal person.

Finally: sick.

Finally.

I needed to be sick just as badly as I needed it to be confirmed. There is no consolation in closed eyes. I wanted to get up and hug Dr. Magnus, but I didn't know the man and all he did was hand me a piece of paper: Venlafaxina (Vandral Retard) and tell me to get looked after. He had to be the one to make to the decree: I was to be considered an urgent case and watched over. As a young woman with a certain comeliness, what would the doctor think if I hugged him and what if he didn't let me come back, then what? Who would sign off that I was sick? Who would be my judge? Besides, I was ill and didn't have the strength for hugging. Or the will. Or the emotion. The self-possession, even. God had heard me. How I had pleaded. My hand had been stamped. It made me very happy to have that authority: I am weak, so weak, sickly, skinny, flimsy, fragile, so fragile. I even started laughing and Dr. Magnus looked at me with mistrust.

You have depression, he repeated.

Depression incubates like an egg, it hatches and brings you to meet its deepest chasms. I adore that Clarice Lispector story in which she observes an egg. The whole entire story is about one egg. In another of her stories, a woman gets on a bus with a box of them and tries not to let any of them break.

Fragility. Integrity.

Clarice and cracked eggs. Clarice and whole eggs.

Clarice and the Philosophy of the Egg. That's what I would title my thesis if I were a scholar. The egg is what is to come. It is present and future. It is geometry and fissure. Depression is a swirling canoe. You just have to get in: you don't even have to paddle.

NIGHTMARE

I am an old woman gamboling in a field.

I find my Communion dress behind a prickly bush. On the tag, someone has written:

ADELAIDA, DON'T RUN SO MUCH.

Sadness bucks protocol and bucks the world. Sadness is a revolution and it unsettles happy people. Sadness is mundane gestures. A swollen eyelid. Sadness is not named. Sadness is learned from forests and creeks: I remember when I studied evergreen and deciduous trees. At the age of nine, in the small-town school, did no one else interpret that as a lesson about ourselves? Parasites. There is a species of duck called the polla de agua—literally, "water cock"—and that made us titter. We were preteens hiding our laughter behind our hands and on that winter day in the 1990s, the natural sciences teacher had the misfortune of turning up in class with swollen pomegranate lips (she'd had an allergic reaction to lipstick), and she left the classroom to get the principal, who was also my father.

We'd only asked if the water cock would be on the test, we hadn't meant to misbehave.

My dad was also my school principal. Double obedience.

Order in the room!

At seventeen, I realized that lips swell a lot, a ton, from kissing someone with a beard. What a discovery. I thought of that teacher, her lovely fat lips: festive.

I am not an evergreen. I don't keep the same leaves throughout the seasons. I'm not rigid, or green, my twigs don't grow, they don't adapt, sunlight doesn't pass through my skull, I don't know how to live without rubbing at my wounds. I don't come under attack from caterpillars. My veins don't show and I'm no good at starting fires. Incidentally, I grew up among carob trees, junipers and pines, known for their ability to withstand anything. They are the Knights of the Round Table: unbreakable, standing honor, branches held aloft. I have climbed them and have tasted their dried sap with the tip of my tongue. It tastes bitter and termites stick in it and die, I think. There is a poem by the Mallorcan Miquel Costa i Llobera about a pine tree that resists, triumphs, and continues to endure. "Lo pi de Fomentor," it's called. One of our Catalan teachers was obsessed with it. Ms. Margarita. She wrote the opening lines on the high school blackboard. She put her zeal into it, her zest for life bristled and nobody paid attention. We whispered. When she turned around and saw our faces, she took her sunglasses out of her purse and went into the hallway to cry. Into the dark hall with her dark glasses. She must have done it some fifteen times. And one day, we never saw her again.

She dissolved into that hall of shadows.

The most primordial sadness I've ever seen was Amy Winehouse's. Talent mixed with cocaine, mixed with familial rootlessness, a jumble of lighters, rhythmic rage, love of words, earthquake on stage, exquisite vulgarity, premonitions in the middle of the night, fried banana sandwiches, impulsive prattle, picturesque make-up, size XXS electric feathers, flying with the breeze, sticking like gum, eloquent high heels. The greater her agony, the higher she made her bun. They mention that in the documentary about her life: her bun was symbolic, an SOS. I've looked online for her peak moment, her highest beehive, Winehouse Everest. A picture of the behemoth beehive: a thousand bobby pins in the wild hurricane of her hair. In most of her photographs, you can glimpse the agony of an almost-living sparrow, of a solitary hen, a malnourished baby. Of a woman who lives in a hurry and gets severely drunk, ten things at once, a shoddily gift-wrapped present from a fan who's been waiting seven hours to see her, heroin in her pocket, worm-eaten anxiety pills, paparazzi in the bathroom, scream, scream, scream, sublime song.

NIGHTMARE

My friend Oriol Tellado is vomiting dirt. A country of dirt. Fertile dirt, which serves as fertilizer, burnt dirt, with seeds. Exotic dirt, Martian dirt, dirt with mummified priests, dirt with glass, dirt with lichen. Dirt with worms. Snowy dirt. After two days of vomiting dirt, he has created a mountain.

From the shape of the peak, it resembles a cave.

FRAME

I discovered the writer Janet Frame this year. If I'm ever asked when I first read her, I'll say without hesitation:

My year of depression.

Depression leaves a bigger mark than a first boyfriend. I will never, ever forget the year I was depressed. The year of my junkie despondency. My life is divided into several stages: before books / after books. Before Mallorca / after Mallorca. Before depression / after depression. Passion, geography, disease.

Frame was a writer who had to go mad to get published. What worried her most was that she had cavities, right there, teeny-tiny ones. Her hair was safety sign orange and frizzy and coiffed upward like an ice cream cone. Odd appearance, painful teeth, freckles scattered willy-nilly, a granite tile. Her presence in the world was strange. She was born incomprehensible, cartoonish, different, and to be born in that way is to bet that you will be kept separate.

Discreet, you know? You draw enough attention to yourself just being how you are.

Camouflage yourself behind the bushes.

She lived her life obsessed with standing out, with publishing, with being seen. Struggle heaped on struggle. The slippery buoy they situate in the middle of the sea. That was Janet Frame. She was diagnosed very early with schizophrenia and wrote *An Angel at My Table* with sparks shooting from her hands. An electrifying book. I read it while they gave me shocks: it blew a fuse.

"If the world of the mad were the world where I now officially belonged (lifelong disease, no cure, no hope) then I would use it to survive, I would excel in it. I sensed that it did not exclude me from being a poet."

RETWEET

"Life is shit. You can always die, all the time, even at Christmas. One day you die and that's it: a ton of people crying. It doesn't matter how much you love, how much you are loved: nothing can keep you here.

"We're going to take good care of each other, give each other kisses, and do whatever the hell we feel like."

Lorena G. Maldonado. @lorenagm7

OFELIA X

While on the red pill (still talking about Vandral Retard), I could barely walk. Or talk. One day I had to cross the street and I decided to throw myself in front of a car. I chose a black one. I suppose the majority of suicidal people choose that color. Or red, for the Devil. Or yellowish, rot. I waited for a few to pass. Well, to be honest, I was standing there for an hour: analyzing engines, roars. Black cars passed with kids in the backseat. I'm not that sadistic: I needed to die, but children are blameless. Children are untouchable, and if I have one mission in life, it's not to harm them.

Not a scratch on the kids.

Or animals.

To the adults, I know I've hurt you and ask for your forgiveness. Forgive me, I said quietly on the sidewalk, thinking about suicide.

Big apology.

Of the biggest and most serious things that depression has taught me, it's to say I'm sorry (easily). A thousand apologies to all. Sorry if you don't like my books. Sorry if I am excessive in love, in hate. Sorry if I don't communicate well or if I communicate too much. Sorry for the cheating, lovers, boyfriends, teachers, friends. Sorry for the omissions, the forgetfulness, being late. Sorry for not screaming sorry when I should have screamed it. For the lies, I don't want to think about them. Sorry for the boring chitchat at the table and the cold coffees. And for losing my grip and mouthing off. For the faux pas. For the competitiveness. Sorry for the distance: a person changes. Sorry for the caresses you didn't like, the sentences that escape my mouth, for what cannot be undone and for the fried eggs with too much oil. I'm sorry, for real, at the top of my lungs, my throat doubles under the weight of such sincerity: I serve it to you feverish, my candor, I give it to you boisterous and zany and in an intelligible vial, because I have nothing left to lose. Sorry for the headwind, I wasn't careful enough to stop it with the palm of my hand. Sorry, too, for the wind that caught us off guard and stopped an important conversation, left us, how were we? Strange, mute: and now what?

What do you say after the wind?

The wind is impertinent, it doesn't listen. Sorry in the midst of this storm.

Sorry from the flintiest part of my being.

I felt horrible, horrible, worse than ever, and it wasn't just the physical pain I felt—a piquant anemia—it was the dryness in my mouth, my whisper like a weed, considering the senselessness of the planet. Don't let the children see, cover their eyes (I'm so protective, more and more like my mother). I plucked dead skin off my lips and kept the pieces warm in my hands, rolling them into little balls as red cars, green cars, silver cars drove by. I didn't care that I looked unattractive two seconds before my first suicide attempt. I don't admit to unattractiveness even in a commissioned piece of flash fiction. I was about to get into position when a bum walked by, stuck on one sentence: This damn sun that is killing me, and he continued muttering vaguely, *h* sounds, lots of *n*s, some vowels, whatever: nananana. The bum was dragging a cart, so slow, such a nuisance, what's he ferrying around with such prudence in that corroded contraption: bursts of light? It's so hard to kill yourself, godammit! Nobody lets you. When it isn't one person, it's another. Can't you all stay inside your homes, annoying people, nice and quiet? Suddenly, there at a distant traffic light, I spotted a black car with a man on his own: sweaty, sleeves rolled-up, bad day to invest in the stock market, half-a-Xanax look on his face. The windshield with a smattering of seagull crap, fluorescent inspection sticker, a fast car. Perfect. I had no doubt my fate was near. It was the perfect car to run me over, but I didn't move. Shit, Almudena! I don't know why the image of a cat spinning around on a microwave plate came to mind but when the vision ended, I was disproportionately aware of myself: the hairs on my arm, stiff. My very uncomfortable legs, my chatty summer sandals, my glistening belly and the empty, claustrophobic stomach below it: I wanted to be free of the body that represented me. My mind was dead. All that was left was to obliterate the body. I blamed myself for all the past damage: all of it, all of it, all of it! A guilt pile-up in my brain. Whistles. A nocturnal caw, but it's histrionic midday! Can't one vomit up guilt? Excise it? The people who had hurt me did so because I deserved it. I wasn't capable of managing my own money. Besides, I was a fucking mooch. One day I considered becoming a prostitute.

In secret: blue contacts and fishnets.

Blowjobs would be better than fucking: faster. With a lot of booze and thinking about the literature I liked. Money, after all, easy money, dizzy bills. No more debts.

I don't owe you people anything!

Just lovely.

You have to be selfish to commit suicide. Forget who and what loves you, lock away affection, love, sweetness, generosity, laughter, draw the bolt, and goodbye. I jumped in front of a black car. Late, and poorly, because he braked. That businessman, wait, he wasn't a businessman, I think he worked in real estate, he had a nametag on, claimed his heart was racing and an unusual rage pooled in his eyes. Typical. And what the fuck was I trying to do and why had I chosen him, what was this hex that had pursued him since the previous month: losses, losses, and more losses, reprimands one after another. It had been insane, a nightmare, a huge drag, and now you. Typical. Did I have a family, could he take me to a doctor, to the planetarium, to a neighborhood meeting or something? What is recommended in these cases? And I said something about Dr. Magnus, that Dr. Magnus took care of me with kind words and energizing drugs, though he wasn't there now because Dr. Magnus wasn't always there and he has problems too and thank you for braking and I'm sorry, I'm sorry for jaywalking, it was an accident and thank you a thousand times, I am infinitely sorry and this and that, it's just that my mind is poisoning me and the office worker or whatever he was got back inside his car, though not before moving out of the middle of the street with a shove and a sigh.

Sorry if I'm being rude.

And he had a coughing fit.

And I'm sorry, again. Oh, geez, and now you're coughing. Here, I think I have a cough drop. Do you want it?

After the incident, I went to my partner's house for lunch. For him to help me eat lunch. We weren't living together yet. He opened the door and I hugged him, in tears. I didn't tell him anything, except that the walk had been really long.

Outrageously so.

And that depression was hitting me hard.

Like steel. Depression was me.

The street where I'd flipped: Ofelia X.

NIGHTMARE

Two kidnappers lock me in a secret chamber. The place reminds me of the spaceship in the first *Alien* movie. The sliding doors open and they toss me a ball of yarn.

I start to unravel it.

It's my only entertainment. And it is endless.

RETWEET

"Almost all of my ills are cured by sleeping."
    Francisca P. @franciscapageo

SIDE EFFECTS

After a year of crying every day, you stop knowing why you cry. Why anything. You don't even care. It isn't incumbent on you, it slips away, you are a bowling lane, it slips and it slips, period. You are repulsed by medical knowledge. Dr. Magnus is pure window dressing. You go there as if to cling to someone. So he will keep affirming that I'm sick, given that, fuck, I'm really sick. And all the people around you: so embarrassing. The smilers. You don't work anymore, right? Much less write. Ah, well that has a name: disability, we declare you a disabled bookworm. What a shame: and we thought you had talent. One less participant in the broken-down tractor race. You don't know how to pronounce the word *depression*: it frightens you more than the Holocaust, everything is excessive, the world asks you to walk, to sing, to dance, to write and the world is poorly made, let's start there.

I have identified with the sole of a shoe.

Crying heals a specific psychological pain, but depression is an arrow embedded, where? Well, nowhere, if only there was a specific place. An x-ray. A blood test. A lump. It is an arrow embedded in you, invisible. It rusts over time and there I am with the obligation to try to make the emptiness something solid. I show a little bit of thigh to my friends: I can feel it here, the depression, but yesterday it was my neck tingling. I look for a mad accomplice who will understand the terror of the emptiness inside the void. It hurts worse every day. It's the same relationship one has with the dead. They appear, you reject them, they appear again, you keep them in your memory or you ask them to go to back to their graves. Leave like the well-behaved dead and forget you, dissolve.

The dead, dissolved in hydrochloric acid.

Leave me alone here, puerile and cold, please.

That's how depression shows up, just to be clear. The ringing of a Japanese gong.

Living with depression is living with a dead person on your back. Conversing with him. Showering with him. One morning I got in the shower and I almost managed to wash my whole body, but I was met with superhuman force that blocked me from rinsing my hair. I lathered with shampoo and then had to stop. My hair, sudsy and white, was putting up a fight. I couldn't rinse it out because I was not capable of lifting my right arm while holding the handheld shower head: it weighed a hundred pounds. I stayed like that. Wet. Shivering from cold, from fear, from cold. I think I cried out:

Just kill me already!

A whole morning. Naked and useless. Shampoo in my hair. Crying. You are factory defective.

A dead man was watching me, I know it. From overhead.

There are basements we have to keep locked. Depression makes you a sleepwalker, it kills you. It is a constant state of panic. You now have an unexpected enemy who does not leave, does not leave, doesn't go and doesn't say: give me all the drugs on the planet. There are only two options when it comes to covering over depression, two genuine kinds of rest: Sleep or death.

One afternoon, I was clinging to the couch. Arms bound. Intense clinging. The couch is the depressed person's coffin. Their vessel. You sail in it. Sleeping, waking, thinking, crying. The days pass. Well, one evening I was in that mode and because of not getting up to go to the bathroom, which was (truly) very nearby, I almost pissed myself and I felt out of my body. Small. Baby. Curled. Feeble. Prohibited by the same superhuman force that had impeded me from rinsing my hair in the shower: a malignant power prowls brains, watch out.

Drugs don't help at the start of depression: they accentuate the physical discomfort. They are made of steel. It takes time for the body to assimilate them. They don't sit well. You yawn thirty-seven times a day, even with a UFO touching down in the backyard. Food is disgusting, it tastes like metallic plum. The only thing I ate with any interest was melon and in winter there are hardly any melons, which was why my Aunt Antonina ran around half of Madrid in search of a melon and brought me back one from Alcobendas, cradled in her arms like a newborn.

Didn't you want melon? Well, here's your melon!

Piel de sapo, the sticker said. Toad skin. It seemed absurd to me, a toad-skin melon. Amphibian melon. Stuff that wouldn't have occurred to me before. That a melon had toad skin made me more depressed.

I cried over it: toad skin, toad skin, I was inconsolable.

Months later, I started enjoying chocolate: a return to child-hood. In the beginning, I wanted to get sick from malnutrition, to destroy myself before depression ordered me to. Get ahead of the disaster. And for it to be a real disease: malnutrition, not depression. Anorexia, not depression. Dementia, not depression. I would rather have had pneumonia, tuberculosis. A plateful of food was a challenge, sleeping was another, talking was a blinding challenge, loving someone: impossible. And for them to love you, to love you with that pity, that's the stuff of the lionhearted.

The real truth.

One who loves you when you have depression deserves a Garden of Eden. A cloak of flowers upon waking. A holiday on the most comfortable cloud in the sky. A soft kiss, iridescent, fleshy lips, Tropico-Mediterranean flavor, clean autumn sun-light, fresh desire, the privacy of striped parasols, the blink of a breeze, the perfect duration to want it to last until the hereafter.

A teenage kiss; that's what I was getting at.

So many people took care of me. How many apologies awaited me after my miserable scarecrow breakdown. I needed a pause so as to begin to remount, an Olympic gymnast-size remount: I was apprehensive, I couldn't see it clearly, it was a utopia, an incommensurable feat. Depression needs cushions, soft spaces, technological order. One couch at home where I could be sick and another couch in Dr. Magnus's office where I could get better.

SOLOMON

I bought the Bible of Depression. I brought it with me to the Hostal Sinatra and it took a huge effort to get it there, since my arms can't even bear the weight of a spotted ladybug. The Bible is called *The Noonday Demon: An Atlas of Depression* by Andrew Solomon. Besides reading his (exceptional) book over the course of a year, I've watched the author discuss his research on YouTube. I read him and had the sense that he had become my second psychiatrist: there was Dr. Magnus, my in-person therapist, and there was Andrew Solomon, therapist online. In the YouTube interviews, the author insists that we who suffer from depression have a very battered truth: an absolute faith, a cyclical delusion lying to us on the inside. Depression is a liar. A Machiavellian whirlpool.

In his talks, Solomon reflects: I know it's a contradiction that's hard to assimilate, but even the truth lies. That we one day die is a truth (you don't have to argue this point with a sick person) while, at the same time, it's a lie. It is an unsustainable truth because we have wonderful plans this afternoon which tip our fear to one side of the scale: we are still alive. Let's dance.

We're in dialogue, *The Noonday Demon* and me. It took me a while to get the book. The Spanish edition is seven hundred pages long and I found it imposing, such a round figure, so terribly exact. It includes a glossary of medications. But it's no know-it-all, brash memoir. It meets my eyes with terror, with sweetness. It never ends. It's heavy, incredibly thick, and I carried it around from café to café and measured my life force with it: if I could lug that sagacious rock so far, to all those faraway cafés, if I could read it without crying in view of other, happy people who watched me with concern, it was because I was becoming a regular person, run-of-the-mill, normal.

I couldn't have read Solomon in the early months of illness. Nor bear its triple weight: intelligent, nutritive, empathic.

"Depression is the flaw in love." And he goes on: "To be creatures who love, we must be creatures who can despair," hearkening back to William Styron's "despair beyond despair." I don't think I'll ever forget the discovery. I've lost count of my one thousand favorite definitions of this mawkish disease. Stubborn and deceptive: one day you feel like you're close to being well and the next you feel like a bullet-riddled buzzard. It is an emotional revolution. Neither rational nor irrational. It's like those personalities that are built around a calcified trauma. It's changeable: it depends on the tooth it bites you with, on the orders from a sallow brain, on the insignificance inside the void. You don't know what will happen: every day is an awful surprise.

It's somebody pulling; pulling poorly, rakishly. Namelessly.

About drugs Solomon states:

"Every morning and every night, I look at the pills in my hand: white, pink, red, turquoise. Sometimes they look like writing in my hand, hieroglyphics saying that the future might be all right and that I owe it to myself to live on and see. I feel sometimes as though I am swallowing my own funeral twice a day as, without these pills, I'd be long gone."

Swallow a funeral at night. Our stomach hangs in there, fire-proof: depression is the synonym of toxicity. One time I dreamt I was thief who specialized in stealing fire extinguishers. With a big sack and everything. And my mask. I ripped them out of public places: any kind, any shape. As the dream progressed, it turned out my stomach caught fire and I used the extinguishers to put it out: a fulminating squall.

DR. MAGNUS

It's a well-known response, our taking exception to psychiatrists, shielding ourselves from them. Movie, tv, radio talk show hosts, parents, grandparents, and officers of the law all told us: just say no to drugs.

And to shrinks.

Dr. Magnus has presence, he leaves the space of five and a half hugs between us. He listens to me closely, but from a distance. With his psychiatry degree, he has managed to bring me back to life with prescriptions for serotonin. I've watched him calculate: how much serotonin for x amount of melancholy. How much Zolpidem for x amount of anguish. How many words for x distress. How much lithium for x rage. How many sentences, how much attention for x exhaustion. How much x for my circulatory system. How much x so I will walk and not stand still on the sidewalk. How much x so that I don't look at a car longer than three seconds, and all this while I writhe on the couch.

What's wrong?

Do I tell him this? Do I tell him that?

All calculations, poetic calculations.

My depression has been his depression. He has interiorized it. He solves matrixes and Gauss bells for me. I find math absolutely terrifying.

Philosophy calms me, calm thinking.

I'm not made for solving, just elucidating.

Dr. Magnus has thought and solved. He truly dislikes depression. Mine, I suppose, and that of other patients. It disturbs him that there is depression in the world. I see it. I glean it from the way he writes the prescription. With a strangled pen. In capital letters. Forceful. I am reminded of something from the 80s, he is the Ghostbuster of my depression. The concern with which he writes his diagnosis runs through the official square. Gravely wounded ink. The penmanship of a psychiatrist-warrior:

Venlafaxine, help Almudena.

I haven't done talk therapy. Not with a professional. A psychotherapist, psychologist, nothing. Taking regulated drugs has been my only medicine. I've talked for hours with Antonina, with my partner, with my cat. Everything is therapy, Dr. Magnus underscores in one of our sessions: what you have gotten out of this and what you have told others. Your book. Your writing. You yourself, changing.

In the beginning, in his office, I hardly spoke. I sat in the corner of the couch in a heavy sweater and Dr. Magnus launched questions into the dramatic air accumulating in the room. In case I answered one. There were four or five tragic sessions, grating, which felt eternal, and even he interrupted the faltering conversation and left the room to get my aunt, who he found reading in the dark, just to calm the storm in the atmosphere.

A breath.

Over the course of two months, I gradually improved. A year after stepping into his office, we now discussed current events, I sent him copies of the first chapters of this book and he went out of his way to praise them. He agreed to be Dr. Magnus and in his emails he started to sign off as such: *Hugs, Dr. Magnus*. We got on great in terms of our sense of humor, mutual understanding, respect for Rafa Nadal, the depth of our sentences, breakneck emotions.

I still go to his office. My Aunt Antonina accompanies me and gives me a gentle push. I am a person with enough strength to stomp on the world. I am fortified with joy: we have cleared away the ash that was making me so sick and killing me slowly. We laugh during our appointments. Sometimes he tells me not at all pleasant things that have happened in his life. Others are better. And we share our opinions on daily life: whether we like Christmas or playing with kids. I ask him about his profession.

Is it very difficult to bear other people's sadness?

We change roles.

It's an odd friendship, medicinal.

ENCOUNTER

Smack dab in the middle of transoceanic depression, I met up with Cristina B. We aren't very close and have never told each other secrets. We made plans to meet in an outdoor restaurant which has since gone out of business. We are a generation unaccustomed to seeing each other in the same bars as always. Establishments change or close or are destroyed by debts or bank loans.

Nothing stands for long: we move around—now here's a graphic image—on our knees. Kneeling millennials. The trees watched us from above and pinecones crunched on the rooftops, it was the start of autumn and the sky was expanding in persuasive colors that made us stay there the whole evening together, beers in hand. Cristina B. is gorgeous and she arrived three minutes after I'd sat down to curse the beauty of the park. Beauty of perfumed helicopter! She arrived in a hurry, moving inside a floating, strappy dress. She was exultant, kissed by the lovely rays of the sun.

I am exultant, she confirmed.

We talked about our summers. She had spent the summer months away from Madrid, in a not-yet-fashionable Andalusian seaside village that still retained small virgin coves and cosmic silence. Do you remember the sea of the 90s? Well, it was like this: a blend of blues, cobalt, indigo, navy. Orange and maroon stars sticking to the rocks and one old joint to share between the three of us. So funny. I laughed a lot those nights: we cracked each other up, my boyfriend and my friend and I. God, we were so funny. But it sucks because Queen Letizia's started summering there—just wait until next year: it will be overrun with tourists, so gross, they should just take their yacht and go to the Maldives. So true. Royalty is totally pointless.

I don't know how I started telling her about my depression. I was inspired by her zest for life; we were opposites, squared. She was stunning and I was downcast, and I sensed that it wouldn't crush her if I started talking about my mental state. Not her. It had been months since I'd observed such a concentrated radiance in one person. Our conversation wouldn't flag, neither would the youthful ardor, and we were surround by the best sunset in the last ten years. And in the background, deep in the background, the last cicada of summer, submerged in its insect hunger, released an atavistic whistle.

Cristina B. untangled the ends of her hair, which shone between her fingers. She had grown a voluptuous mane in no time at all. I imagined taking her picture and titling it: *Cristina B., Sea Nymph.*

She wasn't exactly surprised to hear about my depression. She knew people who had been through it. At university she had a housemate who, when driving, wanted to kill herself on every curve. She drove alongside cliffs. And she would arrive back at the flat and announce: Fifty-two curves and I'm still here, I wanted to kill myself fifty-two times in one hour. She was a fabulous girl: twenty-two, attractive, good grades, no problem hooking up, had money. She had everything, you know? It's like happiness had no impact on keeping the disease at bay—it catches up to you and BAM, right?

In spite of happiness. Bam, that's right: bam, I repeated.

Cristina B. made a pistol with her fingers: bam, bam.

But seriously, all joking aside: such voraciousness, she concluded.

The waiter at the bar in decline brought us a bowl of pistachios and we set to eating them, playing with the shells.

I was starving. You don't even get a tapa with your beer anymore.

I tried to kill myself. Jumping in front of a car, I said in a sudden attack of honesty.

Cristina B. looked at me for a second—God she was radiant!—brushed aside a pistachio shell and asked:

Which street? (This question, I understand, was owed to the fact that we live in the same Madrid neighborhood).

Ofelia X.

She smiled and joyfully declared:

Shit, Almudena! You could have picked a more glamourous street!

I thought that was funny. We mocked my craziness a bit. I'd never thought I'd be able to laugh at my depression. At my attempted suicide. Not by a long shot. And I saw myself there, confronting it, with a beer I liked and a companion dripping in floral essences, *joie de vie*. In a scene so beautiful it was hyperbolic. That day, I understood what it was to come back, come back out of pleasure, come back for real, abruptly, in between catharsis and the thrill of knowing I was coming back and that, as a friendly man lost in the area suggested:

There's hope, right?

There is hope!

RETWEET

"To cry over something and use that cry to cry about everything else: the economics of crying."
    nuri. @nocioncomun

SLAM

I'm a slamming door. The first door I slammed as a teenager, the last door I slammed in my room in Mallorca and the doors I slam now (the slams originate in my trachea, here comes one now!) and the doors I'll slam as an old woman with an ill-tempered cane and the Aristotelian wrinkle that will form between my brows from all the imagining of dream books, books errant.

Present, past, future, old age combined into four slams of the door.

To be more precise: I am the air produced by the slam, the tiny dust particles left behind by a furiously slammed door. The remnants.

I will die while writing the word *scorch*.

New doors. Various slams. Keys that come and go. Partners: blond, tall, dark, going grey. A deep crack at the corners of my mouth. Moves west: a park observes us, a swingset attacks. Apartments that are yeses and nos and I'm-not-sures, but let's not think twice: we have to live, right? Let's live! An outsider's fight (with lance, pencil, or catapult) to be a real authentic Mallorquina. Shutting the door in a rage, in raptures, in flames, injustice licking at my lungs, straining the skin of my throat, all writing begins there, in the larynx: it is a disagreement—a painful one—with the world. A scramble of quivering words that I expel, I unleash, vibrating on the page that observes me in its blankness. You have to undress the words. And the page waits, so very blank, so empty that it disturbs me. Gives me a bad feeling. And it doesn't go away. I am, *a priori*, a projectile of wild wind, of wooden door, of damaged home.

And an inaudible creak. Silence and shouting, simultaneous.

A door's best way to express itself is with a slam and thus I congratulate myself: I have curbed myself and then released my childishness (trinkets! trinkets!) in every slammed door of my existence. The atmosphere left behind is an uncertain one; swift, hostile, but purified. Slamming doors has saved me and books have saved from me an invisible adolescence, dun-colored, with no real helping hand and in the back of the classroom, because I don't know if you are nearsighted, ungrateful, or autistic, but in any case: you're no good.

The best thing is for you to go the Arts route and prepare for some useless profession. Because you are no good.

To which I would like to reply (I retort from the present, because it's never too late): I'm going to commit myself to the striptease of words, what do you think?

I was prepared to go to high school with a gas mask and wetsuit. What am I saying: a beekeeper suit. I was this close. That fucking school was like a prison for juvenile delinquents, but without the beds. Drugs have just saved me from this depression. Dear, darling drugs: I will gather with them soon. You are all invited to the pharma party we'll hold on a sunset sail with music by Rachmaninov and Cuban pachanga. I've ordered a diving board to be installed and anyone who feels like it can jump and crack their shin: it's not that serious. Nothing is that serious after a little jaunt in the arms of the Devil. I have been liberated, I suspect, from this brutal disease that is depression; a disease that incubates like any virus, in a jar of strawberry jam.

An innocent jar, unarmed.

In a jarful of childhood, it incubates.

And explodes.

The battle begins.

EPILOGUE

I've been okay for a few months now. Still medicated, though. I have a recurring dream: I'm walking down the street wearing very dark glasses. I can't make out any human figures, only circular ones, running red lights, death amongst flashes of white.

I guess that's what I have left. Terror in my conscience. I've defied physical death—when I arrived unconscious at the hospital with a burst tumor on my ovary—and mental, when I confessed to Dr. Magnus that I did not want to be in this world. That I wanted to be erased. That I was searching for immediate methods and quick results and hundreds of ways to kill myself: cars, wires, roofs, overdose, knives.

Well, I was fixated on cars.

Red cars.

Diabolic.

I see myself as self-sufficient, decisive, willful; I don't cry because life goes on and I live inside its subtle gearworks: one day you're alive and the next, you die?

I am watched over by the attentive eyes of family, companions, friends.

Occasionally, something glorious happens: somebody loves me more than usual.

Via my phone and social media, I receive motivational quotes and sun-dappled landscapes. Songs. Poems.

Almudena, have you seen what a wonderful world!

I can eat. On my palate I note substantial flavors, crisp and unprecedented. Feeding myself seems a miracle. I enjoy a beer at a bar. I write, delete, smile. I recognize my weakness and I am stunned by sadness's torrential nature. Weather alert.

When it arrives, it lays waste.

Two years in dialogue with death, stroking its sticky, reckless hand.

I've become close with the worst creature on the planet: the only true enemy. Or in the words of Virginia Woolf: "It is death against whom I ride with my spear couched and my hair flying back." The thing is, that's just it. We aren't bad people, not really. We make mistakes, we don't keep our worst defects in check, we misconstrue specific situations. We will all die in the end, defeated by the only enemy with the strength to subdue us: death, who comes in disguise, says hello, then vanishes into thin air.

Sometimes I pat the body I tried to kill on Ofelia X. A body without ovaries. It shrinks from reality. I'm still standing. I write and I love and I rage and then I'm sweet.

I wrote *Pharmakon* because I thought of nothing but dying.

I had other projects underway, a *nouvelle* about the first sparks of adolescence and a collection of short stories. And I left them half-finished because this mental illness of mine has been absolutely explosive. A reverberation. I miss the clarity provoked by being unmoored.

Mental illness has revved up my intelligence.

I've been inspired by the psycho-phonies of my mind. I've taken whole packs of pills: red, orange, white. I've never been at such a breaking point. And, even though I was at first resistant to medication, they did me good. I've determined that there is a chemical poetry—I've written these pages in an altered state—connected to creativity, which leads to remembering the crossroads in our past.

Embedded moments, cyst-like.

Were they traumatic?

They were impossible.

If I had to make a comparison, I'd say that just as Marcel Proust used the muffin as a time machine, I've taken pills and capsules that have organized my memory. Through sensations and fragments.

I needed to uncover my childhood.

Drugs have been crucial to my healing: they pushed the sled. They've been difficult, too. They don't take effect for a month and a half. They are plagued with side effects. It's hard to get off of them. I split my pills in half:

Half of a half. Soon I will have to break that same pill in half. And the half of that half, in half. How very small a pill is, and how much it harbors within. It gets lost in the lines on my palm.

Dr. Magnus continues to point me toward the horizon.

I try to look to the distance, as far as my eyes can see and where the colors fan out and still cameras capture a sensuous hue between surreal and fantastical, and the photographs develop with fire-stains, darkened at the edges, and a girl pulls a stone from the field, comes across a stick bug, and starts to play.

ACKNOWLEDGEMENTS

To Eloy, who came out of a pharmacy and suggested the title for this book. To my Aunt Antonina, who knows all the fruit sellers in Madrid. To Matilde, who holds me in shadow. To Natali, Agustín, Javier S.S., *Alb*, Mario, and Sandra Patricia, who each pointed out hits and misses with their red pens. To M.J. Codes for voice messages from Madrid, to Yanina for voice messages from Buenos Aires, and to Sol for the thoughtful ones. To the hairdressers and nail technicians in my neighborhood, who dye my hair blonde and fix my nails.